VANESSA
NORTH

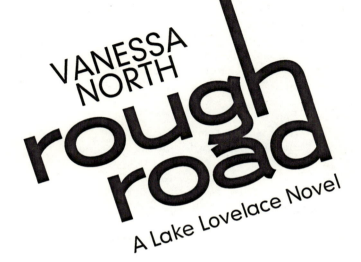

rough
road

A Lake Lovelace Novel

RIPTIDE
PUBLISHING

Riptide Publishing
PO Box 6652
Hillsborough, NJ 08844
www.riptidepublishing.com

Rough Road (A Lake Lovelace Novel)

Cover art: L.C. Chase, lcchase.com/design.htm
Editor: Carole-ann Galloway
Layout: L.C. Chase, lcchase.com/design.htm

ISBN: 978-1-62649-299-8

First edition
September, 2015

Also available in ebook:
ISBN: 978-1-62649-298-1

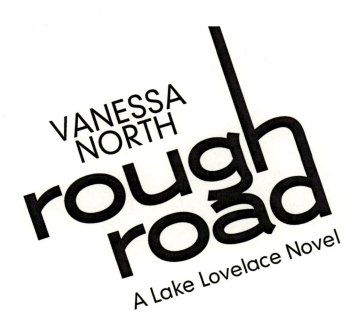

VANESSA NORTH

rough road

A Lake Lovelace Novel

RIPTIDE
PUBLISHING

To #teameddie—I love you guys.
And to Boo and Julio—thank you for the hand-holding,
the beta-reading, and the many ways you boosted my
confidence through the panic-flailing. Friends like you are
everything.

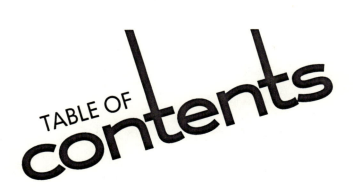

TABLE OF contents

chapter ONE

I'm talking to my best friend, Ben, when the blowout happens. It's so goddamn loud it sounds like a gunshot, and I lose control of the car so fast I'm lucky I don't take out a bunch of other vehicles as I careen off the road. I make one last attempt to correct, barely miss the construction barricade, and end up in the ditch with the airbag in my face, coughing and sputtering.

"Eddie, what the hell was that? Are you okay?" Ben's voice is loud and urgent through the speakers.

"I'm pretty sure I crashed my car, and I'm *dying*, darling." I roll my eyes and gasp for breath, trying to fight back panic with sheer will.

"Where are you? Do you need me to call nine-one-one?"

My car door opens, and a pair of dirty hands pull me back from the airbag and pat my head. "Are you okay? Are you hurt?" A low, rumbly voice fills the car. Not Ben's southeastern drawl, but something more northern, something about the *o*'s is just a little nasal. I blink owlishly into bright-blue eyes below a yellow hard hat. An impossibly pretty, but filthy face. An angel in a fluorescent vest.

"Eddie? Ed!" Ben's voice.

"Oh my god, Ben, angels wear hard hats like in that sex dream I had that time." I wrinkle my nose as the odor of a man who works outside—in Florida, in July—hits me like a brick. "And heaven smells funny."

"Where are you? I'm calling an ambulance."

"Don't bother, Ben," the angel says. "I'll take care of it." Without moving his gaze from mine, he says, "Hang up the phone now, Eddie."

"Yes, sir," I grunt, reaching for the button on the radio. "I'll call you later, Ben." I hang up over Ben's protests.

I look back at the angel, my heart pounding in my chest. "I'm not hurt."

"Airbag deployed; you should probably get checked out. I can call an ambulance, or I can drive you over to the medical center in my truck. You're also acting a little funny."

"No, lovely, that's how I *am*." I draw the last word out long and slow, and I drop a wink on him, jutting my chin just so. Stiff and wobbly, I collect myself from the car and lean against the side of it in the Florida heat, fanning my face with one hand. "Oh my gawd. This heat shouldn't be legal."

"You're lucky you didn't hit the barricade." He nods toward the construction area, where a bunch of men in hard hats like his watch us, their expressions somewhere between amused and concerned. Reaching into my car, he pulls out my phone.

"You want me to call an ambulance? Or should I drive you?"

"You *should* get back to work." I gesture at his coworkers.

"*You* shouldn't worry about me. You happened to run off the road in the middle of the shift change. Don't worry, no one's going to have a problem with me making sure you're okay."

I shake my head. "I don't need a babysitter. I need to call roadside assistance for a tow."

He inspects my car carefully. "You're probably going to need a little bodywork in addition to the new tire. My brother does that sort of thing, if they don't handle it at the dealership."

"Oooh, there are two of you? Is he gay?"

My angel snorts and starts dialing my phone. He mouths the word *Ambulance* at me, then he explains the situation to the dispatcher, including that I seem alert and aware but possibly disoriented. After he hangs up, he scrolls through my address book until he finds roadside and calls them. "He'll leave the keys with me. Come over to the barricade and ask for Wish. Yep, I'll be there."

"I'm not leaving you my car keys!" I hiss.

"Relax, Eddie. I'm not going to steal your busted up S-Class." He rolls his eyes. "Maybe before you crashed it, but now? *Pffft.*" He winks, a slow, deliberate mimicry of the wink I'd given him minutes before.

For what may be the first time in my life, I'm actually at a loss for words. He *sassed* me. *He* sassed *me.*

"What kind of a name is 'Wish'?" I grumble, reaching for my phone, but he holds it out of reach, tapping something on the screen. He'd best not be looking at my photos. Except the selfie I took in the mirror at the gym; I don't mind if he sees that one. I try to remember if there are any dick pics on there. Well, if there are, he's welcome to look at those too.

"Short for 'Aloysius.'" He draws the name out, emphasizing the third syllable. He hands me my phone, screen locked.

"Your mama's a Primus fan? I probably have ties older than you."

"My family is very Catholic." He shrugs. "I wasn't named for Mud."

"Okay."

Sirens are ringing in the distance; they must be for me. "You can take my keys."

"I know." He smiles. He's got a gorgeous smile, teeth a little crooked in a totally endearing way. He's breathtaking, and for a heartbeat, I wish I were twenty years younger. Oh, the trouble I'd have gotten myself into for this one.

When the medics arrive and start checking my vitals, Wish tells them I seem disoriented. I start to argue, but they have me sit on the stretcher in the back anyway. It's nice and shady, much nicer than standing in the sun, so maybe disoriented isn't so bad.

"Text me later; let me know you're okay." He points to the phone in my hand. "I put my number in your address book."

I nod, suddenly exhausted. "Thanks for babysitting me."

He grins, waves, and goes back to work.

I unlock my phone and scroll through my contacts until I find his name, not under Aloysius, but under "Wish." I study it for a long moment.

Wish "my-brother-isn't-gay-but-I-am" Carver

Well. Isn't that lovely?

I text Ben from the hospital. The two of us have spent too many years taking care of each other for me to let him worry.

I'm fine. They're checking me out to make sure I don't have any internal injuries or whatever. I'm okay though.

I stare at the edge of the bed, listening to the clock ticking on the wall. A flat-screen by the ceiling has Fox News on mute, closed captioning covering the headlines at the bottom of the screen. *Boring.* I'm so very bored. Stillness does not suit me.

My phone buzzes.

Good. What about hard-hat-wearing angels?

Oh, what about them? No denying the man was hot. The stubble on his face had been dark, but his eyes light blue. Pretty. But . . .

Too young, I tap out.

I can almost hear Ben laughing when I get the next text.

You say that about all the boys.

I snort. I said it about Ben's partner, Davis, a time or two, but thank goodness Ben didn't listen to me.

Seriously. If he's approaching thirty, it's from a distance.

A young red-haired nurse comes in, checks my eyes for god-knows-what, then points at the TV on the wall. "Want me to change the channel, sweetie?"

I shake my head. "No thanks, love." I hold up my phone as it buzzes again. "Nosy matchmaking friends are keeping me plenty entertained."

She laughs and pats my knee. "All right. You holler if you need anything, okay?"

"Yes, ma'am."

Another text from Ben flashes across my screen.

Do you need a ride?

Oh baby, do I ever. Even though I know it's not what he meant, I let myself imagine sex with Ben. Not the awkward, too-gentle sex we'd fumbled our way through plenty of times—in over twenty years, we'd tried enough to know for sure we weren't compatible—but my fantasy sex with Ben. Rougher. Dirtier. A hand pinning me down, a threat of violence. It's a nice fantasy.

Maybe. I'll let you know.

Or maybe I'll text my hard-hat angel. There was an implicit invitation in the way he'd made it clear he was gay. Sure, he's too young to date, but a hookup wouldn't be entirely unwelcome.

Ah, fuck it. I scroll to his name in my contacts and call him.

"Hello?" I notice that nasal *o* again, and I mean to ask him about it—later.

"Wish, this is Edward Russell."

"Who? Oh, Eddie S-Class. Sorry." He chuckles, a low, easy laugh. "Checking on your car? They picked it up about a half hour after the ambulance left."

"Oh." *Right, the car.* "Yes, thanks. That was very nice."

"So, how are you? Everything check out okay?"

"They're still checking me out. I'm hospital-bored."

"Sorry to hear that. I just got home, but it's pretty boring here too. Want company?"

"You'd come entertain a man you hardly know, because he's bored at the hospital?"

"Wouldn't you? Might be fun. Could be a story to tell at parties years from now. Could be a nice thing to do for a guy who's had a shitty day."

Would I do the same? I don't know, but it's flattering he thinks I'm so selfless.

"Well, come on down, then. I'd love the company."

"Gimme half an hour. Will they let me bring you food?"

"It's worth a shot." I *am* a little hungry.

"You like sandwiches? Not a vegetarian?"

"I do, and I'm not."

"Great. I'll see you soon."

It's a little more than half an hour when he comes in, bag of sandwiches in hand. Without the hard hat and construction vest, he appears even younger than I remember. Damn.

"Hey. Still bored?" He cracks a smile and hands me the bag. "I didn't know what you liked, so I got a couple different things."

"That was sweet of you, Wish."

"I'm sweet all over, Edward Russell." The way he leers at me leaves no doubt in my mind the innuendo was intentional. God, to have the body and arrogance of a twenty-five-year-old again.

"How old are you?" I ask, digging in the bag to see what he's brought. Turkey and avocado on wheat or ham and Swiss on rye. Two sodas in cans. I take the ham and one of the sodas and pass the bag back.

"I'm twenty-four. You?"

I almost choke on the first bite of my sandwich. Gah. Twenty-four. Finally, I swallow. "I just turned forty-four. Last month."

"Nice. Happy belated." He raises his can in mock salute. "Is that gonna be a thing? You're going to say I'm too young and you'll stop flirting and feel all guilty?"

Damn it.

"I was thinking something along those lines," I admit.

"Don't." He points. "I don't need or want a daddy, and the only person who decides what's best for me is me."

I start a little at his vehemence. It's surprisingly bossy and self-assured for someone his age. How much experience can he be speaking from? Okay, I've got to stop thinking of him by his age. He might be young and hot, but I've got "sassy old queen" down to an art.

"Well, I don't want a daddy either." I jut my chin. "But I don't usually play in the kiddie leagues."

Just then a lab-coated doctor walks in. "Mr. Russell?" He looks up from my chart and reaches to shake my hand, but drops his when he sees the sandwich I'm holding. I try not to act too guilty. He glances over at Wish and then back at me. "Your son?"

Ouch.

Wish grunts. "His friend."

"Ah. Okay, then." The doctor eyes my sandwich. "You might have asked first, but yes, it's okay for you to be eating."

"I asked his nurse," Wish volunteered. "She said it was fine."

"Okay, well, Mr. Russell, you're going to have significant bruising on your chest and shoulder from the seatbelt, and you'll probably be sore for a few days. Take it easy, and you should be okay. I'm writing a script for—"

I hold up my hand. "No, don't. I won't fill it. I'll just take Advil."

"Okay, sure. Well, the nurse will be in shortly to discharge you. Okay." He pats his pocket absently, gives a brusque wave, and walks out of the room.

Wish dissolves in laughter. When he's collected himself, he grins at me and does a perfect mimicry of the doc. "Okay."

"Okay." I grin back.

The redheaded nurse returns and goes through the discharge paperwork for me. When she's finished, she gives us each a brisk nod and props the door open.

Wish takes the sandwich out of my hand, rewraps it, and returns it to the bag.

"Come on, S-Class. Let's get you home."

"I'm not the car, you know."

He snorts and holds out a hand to steady me as I stand up. "And you're not the suit either. I get it. And I'm not my age or my hard hat."

"Then I would really like a ride home."

chapter TWO

I can see why he's a little touchy about my pretentious car; he drives a beat-up old F-150. I give him directions to my house—it's a god-awful monstrosity of a thing on the lake. I bought it because the price was right, but never got around to remodeling it to something less gaudy and ostentatious. Unlike Ben and Dave's house, which exudes class and charm, mine screams, *Look how much money I have!*

I'm not ashamed of the money.

I *am* a little ashamed of the house. He's going to think I'm an epic douche.

"So, where are you from, Wish?"

"Minnesota."

"And now you're in Florida. Did you get tired of the snow?"

"Mom got sick last winter. My brother was living here already, and he talked her into coming down so he and his wife could take care of her during chemo. She loved it here, so I moved too. No point staying in Minnesota all alone."

"How's your mama now?" I hold my breath.

"She's good. In remission."

I let out the breath. "I'm glad to hear that. When you said 'loved' instead of 'loves,' well, I worried."

"Ha. Well, she doesn't much care for Florida in July."

"The heat has a way of making people ornery." It's part of what I love about living here: the tension bubbling under the surface is sensual in a primal, earthy way. It gets me so fucking hard.

"What about your dad?"

He grimaces. "Remember what I said about being very Catholic?" I nod.

"Divorce in a Catholic home is not pretty. We aren't on speaking terms."

"I'm sorry."

He shrugs. "He made his choices. What about you? You from here?"

"Indeed. Born and raised. That's my house." I blush as I point to the great big stucco thing with the tiled roof. "You can park in the garage if you want, but I need to enter the code to open it."

"Okay." The truck idles in the driveway as I type my password on the touch pad. He pulls into the spot where my Benz usually sits and turns off the engine.

When he gets out of the car, we stare at each other for a long moment. I want to invite him in. I want to climb him like a tree. I *want*. But he's so damned young.

"You don't know me." He gestures toward the door. "And I can see you have a nice place and maybe you're second-guessing bringing a virtual stranger here. I get it. Why don't I go, and then I'll call you later in the week. Fair warning, I'd like to ask you out on a real date."

"No." I shake my head. "It's not about you being a stranger. I'm trying not to think of you as a corruptible young thing."

"Here I thought we were going to finish our sandwiches, and all this time you were planning to corrupt me? Eddie S-Class, I do believe you have a dirty mind."

Oh boy, did I read that wrong. "Oh my gawd." I cover my face with my hands, peeking at him between my fingers. "I'm so embarrassed."

"Mmm. I like it. How would you corrupt me? I mean, I know I'm younger than you, but this ain't my first rodeo. I'm curious. How would you do it?" Okay, maybe not so wrong at all.

"You want me to . . ."

"I want you to tell me, in great detail, the story of my own corruption." He crosses his arms over his chest, leans back against his truck, and watches me expectantly.

God in heaven, he really means it.

"Let's go inside." I reach for the button to close the garage door.

"No."

"No?"

"No. I want you to tell me out here, in your garage, with the door open, where anyone in the neighborhood who happens to be going for a walk can hear you talking dirty. And, S-Class? Make it *dirty*."

I don't know what it is about him that makes me go for it. Maybe it's because he came to the hospital to save me from my own boredom. Maybe because of the teasing nickname. Maybe it's because I haven't had truly awesome sex in long enough that I'm starting to forget what it's like.

Temporary insanity.

I take off my suit jacket, and hang it on the never-used coat hook by the door. My tie is next—I toss it to him as I reach for my cufflinks, which go in the pocket of my pants. I unbutton my shirt slowly, never breaking eye contact. Any minute I'm going to take it too far, and he's going to look out that open garage door and stop me.

But he doesn't. When I hang the shirt with my jacket and turn back toward him, his gaze drops to my shoulder and chest, which are turning purple and black and a dull red. His eyes widen, and he swallows.

I clear my throat. "I'd start by stripping us both naked. Me first, so you can watch."

Reaching for the button at the top of my trousers, I spare a moment to press the heel of my hand against my dick and close my eyes against the rush of pleasure.

"Take it out. Show it to me."

I unzip, pull my cock out, and hold it in one hand like an offering. He examines it for a long time, long enough to make me uneasy, but my semi hardens under his gaze. Finally, he meets my eyes again.

"A dick piercing? I'm feeling a little corrupted already," he teases. "What would you do next?"

I kick off my shoes, push my pants and briefs down my legs, step out of them, and fold them carefully before setting them aside. I turn around as I take off my socks, and wiggle my ass a little for his viewing pleasure. When I straighten up and face him again, he's got one hand pressed against his own zipper. If I cross the garage to him, I'll be naked in plain view of anyone walking by, practically on display. It *really* turns me on. Who knew my exhibitionist streak ran that deep?

The first step is the hardest—moving from the idea of exhibitionism to the reality of it—but then I find myself smirking as I amble toward him. I hurt from the accident, and I'm a little freaked out, but the captivated expression on his face is like a drug.

I reach for his T-shirt, tugging it up to expose that flat twenty-four-year-old stomach.

When his hand claps down on my bruised shoulder, I hiss sharply, meeting the challenge in his gaze. He squeezes—he didn't grab it by mistake. I let my eyes roll back in my head as I exhale, waiting for the pain to cede to pleasure.

"You . . . like that, don't you?" The squeeze becomes a caress as he explores the edges of the still-forming bruise. He digs his fingers in a little under my clavicle and the frisson of delicious agony draws a whimper from my lips.

"Okay, Eddie. This is the point where we go inside and have a talk."

I heard him, and yeah, I know he's right, but now? I want to chase the ache his fingers are tracing along my chest. I lean into that hand, rewarded with a dull throb north of my heart.

"Come on, man. I may only be twenty-four but I know enough about the game you're playing to know we don't do this without talking. In the house, now." He nudges me away from him, sending another jolt through me.

I swallow, pulling myself together. I thought I wanted him before, but now? It's like a madness inside me. I have to have whatever it is he's promising.

Leading him inside, I say, "Just so you know, my house is . . . Well. It doesn't really reflect my taste, you know?"

"You took your cock out in the garage and you think I give a fuck about your furniture?"

Right. Hookup house call, not a date. It's not like I even have a thing against casual sex. I love casual sex. I just can't help feeling like I'm taking advantage of him.

He follows me into the kitchen, and I notice him glancing around, but he doesn't say anything.

"Still hungry?" he asks, holding up the bag of half-eaten sandwiches.

Not for food. I shake my head, and reach for the bag. I stick it in the gigantic-but-mostly-empty refrigerator. Knowing he's watching, I bend over and pull out a couple of water bottles, letting the chill from the fridge wash across my naked skin and pucker my nipples.

He makes an appreciative noise behind me, and I glance over my shoulder. "See something you like, Hard Hat?"

"Oh yeah. Is that another piercing?"

I stand up, laugh, and hand him a bottle. "You want to see it again, we'd definitely better have that talk."

"You like pain."

It's a statement, not a question.

"Yes."

"Sexually, you get off on pain?"

"Yes." *God, yes.*

"Would you want me to hurt you in the course of having sex?"

Ah. There's the question.

"Do I need pain to get off? No. But for me, it's better that way. If it got you off too, fuck yes, I want you to hurt me. But if you aren't into that? No big deal. We could do the vanilla thing, have a nice time, say good-bye afterward, and let that be that."

"That was remarkably uncoy, S-Class."

"I'm forty-four years old. I'm not going to apologize for what gets me off."

"Good. Because hearing you talk about it gets me hard."

Oh, there is a God, and angels really do wear hard hats.

"'Red' and 'yellow' for safewords," I tell him. "I doubt you'll push me hard enough to need them, but if I say 'yellow' — "

"You need a break. You say 'red,' everything stops."

I study him carefully. He's confident, the flirtatious smile back on his lips. Twenty-four years old. What in Hades am I about to do?

"You really have done this before?"

"Eddie, when I walked over to your car to see if you were okay, your welfare was my only thought. Then you started talking about sex dreams and angels in hard hats to your friend, and my curiosity was piqued."

Shoving a hand through his hair, he steps up close to me. We're about the same height, but he's brawnier. He runs his other hand down the center of my chest, then brushes it back up to pinch and pull at one of my nipples before he continues, teasing me all the while.

"When you got out of the car and I could actually see you? So handsome and swishy and wincing in pain, you made me hard. I wanted to fuck you. I wanted to see you wince from pain I inflicted. Not because I thought you'd like it, but because I like it. The fact that you do like it? That it could be more than a jerk-off fantasy?" He shakes his head, then goes on.

"I had a guy I played with in Minneapolis. He was a little older than me, and into paddles and crops. He didn't care for a naked hand on his ass, but every once in a while, he'd let me. I loved that. Skin to skin, my handprint . . ." The hand on my chest slips back up to my bruised shoulder and grips me again. "Would you let me?"

I'm lost for a moment in the sensation of his hand, rough and warm, on my shoulder. Finally, I nod. "Yes. You can slap my ass, my legs, chest, and face. No closed fist though." Oh, I'd love to really brawl with him, but confessing that seems too intimate. Admitting you like pain is one thing. Pain can be sterilized. Violence though, and a sexual craving for it, tends to creep civilized people right the fuck out.

He releases my shoulder and touches my hair, so gentle. "Any other limits I should know about?"

"Breath play is an absolute hard limit. Other than that?" I shrug. "Let's play it by ear."

"Come here." He leans back against my gaudy marble countertop and pulls me into the V of his legs. I resist a little bit to test the waters. He responds by tugging me firmly into place and wrapping his arms around my waist. God, he's strong.

"I should warn you . . ." I put a hand up to stop him when he bends in for a kiss.

"What's that?" He pauses, but doesn't draw away.

"I'm not a naturally submissive guy. Just because you like to inflict pain and I like to take it doesn't mean you aren't going to have to make me."

"Make you?" His eyebrows pull together as he studies me. I can almost see the gears turning. "Like, a rape fantasy?"

I shake my head. "No, but if you're into that we can try it. It's like this: I get off on pain, but I don't get off on taking orders. I sometimes get off on humiliation, but it's not my usual kink—you'd really have to get me in the mood. I'm not a submissive, I'm a masochist. You don't have to force me, but I still might fight you. I don't know why, but I like it like that."

"So if I tell you we're going to go into the bedroom and I want you to bend yourself over my knee and ask for a spanking?"

"I'll tell you to go fuck yourself." I spit the words out, my body starting to hum with adrenaline.

"You say the sweetest things." He picks me up, roughly, and tosses me over his shoulder. It jostles me, sending pain echoing from my bruised shoulder all the way through my torso. My hard cock rubs against his chest, and a moan escapes me.

"Which way is your bedroom?"

"Fuck you."

"I can probably find it on my own." He shrugs, his shoulder jabbing into my gut, and then he carries me up the stairs. He finds my room easily, and he throws me down on the bed and starts pulling his clothes off. The impact jars my shoulder, and fuck if the pain doesn't get me harder. I sit up and start to crawl away from him, but he grabs my ankle and hauls me back, landing a stinging slap on the outside of my thigh.

"Stay put," he grunts, undressing faster.

The next thing I know, I'm flat on my back, and he's on top of me, skin on skin, and it feels even better than the pain radiating out from my chest and shoulder. When he reaches between us and flicks my Prince Albert with a fingernail, I groan helplessly.

"I gotta see that up close," he mutters. Strong hands pin me down to the bed for a moment. "Don't move."

I wiggle around to remind him about that whole not-naturally-submissive thing, a smile curling my lips up at the corners. He returns the smile, placing a hand on my chest and pushing enough to rev that dull ache of a bruise into something sharper.

"Tell me about these piercings," he murmurs, making his way down my body with his hands, dry callused palms raising goose bumps over my chest and shoulders.

"There's not much to tell. I like pain, and fuck me running, a Prince Albert hurts like hell when you get it done. There's a sadist at my friend Keith's BDSM club who's really into cock and ball torture—he suggested it. The guiche ring is a little different, but it aches so nice when you pull on it." *Take the hint.*

Oh, man, does he. He flicks it, hard, then grips it between his thumb and index finger and tugs, sending a shiver down my spine. Then he reaches up to twist one of my nipples, making me arch into his hand.

"There are some—" I gasp as he pinches harder "—clothespins in the drawer."

He opens the drawer and pulls them out, grabbing the lube and condoms while he's in there. "Really, wooden clothespins?"

I smile. Sometimes simple works. "Yeah. I've been getting off with clothespins on my nipples since before I even knew there was such a thing as a nipple clamp."

He studies one before clipping it to his thumb. Together we watch his thumb turn red, then white. I imagine that pressure around my nipples and bite back a whine of anticipation when he pulls it off his thumb.

He starts to play with my nipples—light, teasing touches. A tickle here, then a lick. He blows on the wet skin and then bites my chest above the nipple. The touch of his teeth sends my hips thrusting into the air. Fingertips return to my nipple, twisting, stretching, sensitizing it. Finally, I feel the pinch of the wooden clothespin closing over the skin. The pain is sharp and intense, and for a moment, I feel flushed all over like I'm going to come. He closes a hand around my cock and gives it a quick, rough tug. *Oh god, he's good at this.*

The next clothespin closes over my other nipple and I close my eyes, catching my breath at the sharpness of it, that exhilarating instant when the pinch and swell of pain short-circuits everything else. A fight or flight response sending that wonderful rush of adrenaline through me. I want to fuck, to fight, to crawl out of my skin and into his.

Another tug on my guiche ring, and I snap my eyes open again, drawing in a deep breath—the sharpness in my nipples subsides, leaving me hungry for more sensation.

"Okay?" he asks softly, twisting the end of one pin, giving me exactly what I need.

I nod, my eyelids heavy with lust, my vision bright with endorphins. I feel high and giddy, a thousand contradictions in my body.

"Want to fuck," I say, reaching for his cock. He twists the clothespin again, and my eyes start to roll back.

"Can I fuck you with these still on?"

I nod, anticipating the scrape and pull of being shoved into the mattress chest-first. "Hell, yeah."

He flips me over, hands skimming down my back, spreading my cheeks, tickling the guiche from behind. Then a hard—really fucking hard—swat lands on my ass,

"You are so fucking hot," he whispers, as if he's surprised. "Hot little ass, all pink right here." He slaps again over the same spot, not even trying to soften the blows. I wriggle. A hand spanking seems incredibly intimate right now, with clothespins digging into my chest as he shoves me harder against the bed. He slaps my ass again, the other cheek lighting up with the sting.

"You want me to fuck you? Fill this hot ass with my cock and ride you hard?"

"Fucking do it." I glance over my shoulder at him, and the way he's staring at me, eyes dark, lips open and drawing a ragged breath, something about it makes my own breath catch. He's beautiful, not just pretty, but stunning, and right now, he's all mine, talking dirty and raining slaps of sensation down on my ass.

"Mine." He growls, reaching for the condom.

I close my eyes against the surprise of hearing my own thought from his lips. He spreads my stinging cheeks, then presses into me.

My body fights him at first, though I breathe deep and push back. He hauls me up to my knees and the changed angle makes everything slide just right. His big, warm chest covers my back, and his hand closes around my cock.

"So fucking sweet, Eddie." He whispers into my ear. "Your ass is so sweet." And then he grips my hips in his hands and fucks me hard.

I often dream of rough, raunchy sex, of a lover who treats me like something he wants to break. I fantasize about bruises on my skin and about hiding a bite mark from my friends. I long for someone to fuck me like he's fucking me, slapping my ass and reaching around to twist at the clothespins.

All I would need to come like this would be to close my eyes and let the carnality of the moment take me. His cock pushing against my prostate on each thrust, his hands manipulating the pins on my oversensitive nipples, his teeth sinking into my shoulder.

"Want you to come." He removes the first clothespin and the rush of pain and pleasure as the blood flows back into my nipple is exquisite. He moves my hand down to my cock, and I take the hint, fucking into my fist for him. My orgasm swells in me, building in intensity as he plays with the other clothespin. When I think it will actually kill me, he pulls off the clothespin, and I'm done, shooting between my fingers and shouting incoherently.

He fucks me harder, right through the sensation, and then he's shouting too, his voice mixing with mine in some primal cacophony. Sweaty-man-fucking at its glorious finest.

We collapse to the bed in a tangle of limbs and sticky mess. I'm dimly aware of his hands on my body, rubbing and gentling me.

"That was so good, Eddie," he praises me, running a hand over my chest. "Come here." He engulfs me in a big hug, clutching me to all those hard muscles and kissing my forehead. He trails soft kisses over my eyelids, then leans back and tilts my chin.

I stare at him, see the tentative confusion in his face, then realize what he's about to do just as his lips close over mine.

Jesus.

The kiss is sweet, but the sensual glide of his tongue into my mouth, the whispers of callused thumbs across my cheekbones, they sting something in me, drawing a well of emotion to the surface, and I'm kissing him back, gripping his head with one hand and tasting him. He groans, holding me close and shuddering under my hands. His skin is hot everywhere it touches mine, hot and bare like me. I've never felt so naked, so vulnerably open to another person as I do in this moment.

I drag my lips away and bury my face in his shoulder while I catch my breath. I don't want to see a good-bye in his eyes.

"Can I get you something to drink, honey?" he asks. "If you tell me where to find it, I'll fix something warm."

He's staying. I don't examine the rush of relief that runs through me.

"There's tea in the cupboard above the stove. And an electric kettle."

He disappears for several minutes. I hear sounds from the kitchen, but I lie on the bed and float on the aches and pains still thrumming through my body.

When he reappears, the spicy-sweet scent of my favorite tea precedes him into the room. He smiles, ducking his head. "I put sugar in it, I hope that's okay?"

I give him a boneless nod and start to sit up.

"Whoa." He sets the tea down, pulls on his boxers, and slides into bed behind me, my back to his chest. Placing the cup in my hands, he wraps his fingers around mine to make sure I don't drop it, and holds me while I take the first cautious sip. It's not too hot, and it's sweet, sweeter than I would make for myself, but good. I drink more deeply, then lower the cup to my lap and let my head loll back against his shoulder.

"That was amazing," I tell him, a smile tilting my lips up. "You were amazing."

"It was fun." He kisses the side of my head. "I'd love to do it again."

My heart sinks a little because yes, I would too, but he's twenty-four years old and I'm too old, too jaded for him.

"I don't know whether it's a good idea," I admit.

"Shhhh. Don't think too much," he whispers. "We can talk about it tomorrow. Just let me hold you awhile."

And that I can do. I snuggle deeper into his embrace and sip at the tea, enjoying the warmth flooding my limbs and the achy souvenirs of our lovemaking on my skin.

I wake to the sound of rhythmic breathing—snoring? No. I lift my head enough to see a moving form backlit by gray window light. Yoga. Wish is doing yoga.

I glance at the clock.

"Oh God, you're exercising? At five in the morning? That'll teach me to let a sadist spend the night."

I pull the pillow over my head, blocking out the noises and the light.

My body hurts. Everywhere. And while some of it is a good hurt—I clench my ass cheeks and feel the pleasant sensitivity of a few light bruises—most of it is a holy-fuck-I-crashed-my-car hurt. Which is most certainly *not*.

"Good morning, S-Class." He pulls the pillow off my head. "How ya feeling?"

"Like I smashed up a $150k car with me inside. Ow. I don't know which hurts more, me or my pride."

His hand traces down my naked back. "You want me to call someone? I'd offer to stay, but I have to be at work at six thirty."

"You're as bad as Ben," I grumble. "Morning people." I grab for the pillow, but he holds it out of reach. He really is a fucking sadist.

"Who's Ben? Who you were on the phone with when you cracked up your car?"

"Ugh, now? We have to talk about him *now*?" I peek over my shoulder, and he's smiling at me, all serene like "coffee before talkie" isn't even a thing in his worldview.

"Well, I need a shower, and then I gotta get out of here. But we could meet for dinner later and you could tell me about him then? I'm guessing he's either your brother, a fuck buddy, or a friendly ex."

I groan, and not only because I need to stop this talk of dating before it gets off the ground, but because these days Ben truly is more like a brother than a lover to me. It doesn't even matter that I don't want him that way; it still hurts that someone else is closer to him than I am. But maybe not as much as it hurt yesterday. "He's my best friend. There, nothing to talk about. We—you and me—we can't date, Wish."

His hand pauses its stroking on my back, then resumes again slower, lighter. "Why not? I'm not in the closet, and I would guess you aren't either. We're hot as fuck in bed together, and I like you. I think you like me, or at least, you smile at me a lot, but that could be gas I suppose."

I give an offended snort, but my heart isn't in it, and I end up laughing instead. Damn him for being so sassy and cute I can't help myself. I roll onto my back, wincing in not-sexy pain. "Because, lovely, you are twenty-four years old. I'm nearly twice your age and that creates an awkward power dynamic for me. I like you. I had a great time last night. But you should date someone closer to your own age. Someone in the same stage of life."

He frowns at me. "So this was just a hookup for you?"

Ouch. Not often I get slut-shamed by my own date. Not date. Hookup. Still, I make my voice soft and conciliatory, because I *do* like him, and he needs to understand that it isn't personal. "I don't expect a relationship when I have sex with someone I just met. Especially not kinky sex. A lot of people like us get what we need outside of monogamous relationships. You know this, right?"

He nods. "Yeah, I felt last night . . . it was special. I felt really connected."

"I'm not going to tell you it was ordinary, everyday kinky fuckin'. But it wasn't the start of a relationship. Don't get attached."

"Okay." He shrugs, but his posture is stiff. "I don't suppose there's anything I can say to that. May I use your shower?"

I nod, a lump in my throat, wanting to take back my words. But they were the truth. He shouldn't get attached. This is for *him*, not for me. He can find some sweet young thing like himself, get married, adopt kids. His generation has opportunities I still feel like I'm peering at through a locked window.

When he finishes in the shower, he comes and sits on the bed, fully clothed.

"Thanks for last night, S-Class." He leans over me and presses a kiss to my forehead. "Call me if you ever want to do it again. No strings."

I close my eyes for a long moment while I try to figure out what to say, and when I open them, he's gone. I sigh and pick up my phone to dial Ben.

"Hey, Ed." *Davis.* "How are you?"

"Why are you answering Ben's phone at six in the morning? Oh, Bedhead, tell me he hasn't converted you into one of *them*."

"No, no, I'm still in the snooze alarm club, but I have an early flight this morning. He's in the shower, want me to tell him you called?"

"Where are you going? Why haven't I heard about this?"

"My former business partner is receiving an award. I promised I'd go be his plus one at this banquet."

His . . . yeah, that raises some protective hackles. "His plus one, Bedhead? Is your former business partner gay?"

"No. But his wife is hugely pregnant and on bed rest. It's a thing—preeclampsia or something. I'm the *backup* plus one."

"Breeding is just not natural." I wrinkle my nose. "Fine, tell him I called, tell him I'm all banged up from the accident and won't be there to help with his month-close books, but he can email them to me. He should get with Jerry about some package deals for gear with the sale of wake boats—our gear sales have slowed down. And he can bring me pizza from Portofino's after work. Plain cheese."

"I'll let him know. You okay? Ben got the impression it wasn't serious?"

"Yeah, I am. Only sore all over. And I picked up a very energetic twenty-four-year-old sadist to take advantage of my bruised and battered self, so I am taking the boss man prerogative of working from home."

"Whoa, whoa, whoa. A twenty-four-year-old sad—?"

"Bye, Davis, talk soon!"

I hang up.

I like Davis Fox with his freckles, his dimples, and his daddy's work ethic. I love that the guy loves my best friend. But I don't want to talk about Wish with him until I've told Ben. Because Ben and I loved each other first, and we don't let each other find out important shit secondhand.

And why the fuck was I filing a hookup under "important shit"?

chapter THREE

When Ben shows up with the pizza, he lets himself in. I hear him rummaging around in the kitchen, but my body is so achy, I don't bother getting up.

"Hey, you." He sticks his head in my bedroom door. "You okay?"

I drink in the sight of him. Ben's handsome in that hard-bodied, brawny way so many athletes are. He tends to fill a space with his presence and then steal your heart with a bashful little-boy smile and a few choice crude words. When we were young, and I had a huge crush on him, that smile was devastating. Now it's really fucking welcome.

"Darling." I throw the back of my hand against my forehead. "Be a dear and bring me some Advil, okay?"

"They didn't give you anything stronger?" He's offended, bless his heart.

"I didn't take the script. You know I don't keep stuff like that in my house."

His nostrils flare and his lips get white around the edges. Ben might be easygoing, but he does have a temper at times. Usually when I'm smothering him.

"You didn't take the script."

I debate telling him he's cute when he's mad, but decide not to fan those particular flames today. "Darling—"

"Because of me?" His eyes are flat and hard.

"Well . . ." Of course because of him. Because for over a dozen years, I've kept my house a narcotic-free zone for him. Because my home should be a safe place for my best friend, and . . . Oh shit, did I say all that out loud? Ben's face is getting redder and redder, and he's balled his hands into fists.

"Oh, for fuck's sake, Eddie." He scrubs a hand over his face. "You shouldn't be in pain because you're worried about *me*."

I fold my arms across my chest. "Well, I'm not going to stop worrying about you. It's what I do. And don't forget, I like pain." I regret it the second it comes out of my mouth. Ben doesn't understand masochism, and he doesn't like the idea of me suffering on his behalf. Equating the two, however tangentially, has led to some of the biggest fights of our decades-long friendship.

"You need to stop acting like I'm your responsibility. I'm a grown-ass man."

"I know this." I look away. I *do* know it. But when you love someone, you want to take care of them, at least, that's how it works for me. *Shit.* I peek up at him and bat my lashes like a starlet. "Oh, Ben. Old habits die hard, but I'm fine. Advil is plenty. It's only bruises. I've had worse after a night at Keith's club. Seriously, I'm fine."

He sighs. "Do you want to come downstairs and eat your pizza? I set the table in the kitchen."

"That sounds lovely."

He paces out of the room, hands still twitching like he wants to wrap them around my neck. I pull on my robe and follow.

After washing up at the kitchen sink, I grab us each a Coke from the fridge. He grunts out a thank you when I hand him one, and I figure we're good.

"So." He spears me with a glare as I'm lifting the first slice of salty-cheesy goodness to my mouth. "What's this I hear about a twenty-four-year-old sadist?"

I set the pizza down. "My hard-hat angel gave me a ride home from the hospital. And then he gave me a rough ride once we got here. It was hot, and it was fun, but that's that."

Ben nods thoughtfully. "You're really not gonna see him again?"

"No."

"Why not?"

What is it about people in committed relationships that makes them want to see everyone else paired off?

"Because he's twenty-four years old, that's why not."

Ben leers. "And I bet he's got stamina for *days*."

Oh, *hell*.

"I'm not gonna lie, that thought has merit. But Ben, you know I don't date younger men. They all seem to want a daddy, and I can't be bothered with that mess." I start eating again, hoping he'll take the hint.

"Mm-hmm." He sprawls back in his chair, resting his soda can on his abs. "Your loss."

"What do you care?"

He shrugs. "I don't. Just making small talk."

"You and I, we don't make small talk," I remind him. "You got something to say?"

"Dave asked me to marry him."

The funny thing about surprise is that it hits like physical pain. A wrench in the gut, a stab behind the eyes, vision and hearing clouding over for a moment, and then it's gone, leaving you wondering whether you had a cardiac event or if your best friend just told you he's getting married.

"He—" I shake my head. *Married*? "I'm sorry, did you say—?"

"I'm getting married."

Definitely a cardiac event.

"I don't know what to say."

"Congratulations is usually the thing." He smiles, a big bright smile. God, I love that smile. Holy shit, he's getting married.

"I— Congratulations." I take another bite of my pizza. *Married*.

"Wait-a-minute. Is Kinky Eddie actually speechless?" he teases. "This has to be a first."

He ain't kidding. "Darling, you don't spring a big announcement on someone. I'm in delicate health." That's the only thing to explain why my heart is racing.

"Delicate health, my ass. I shocked the shit out of you."

"Don't be crude." I study my plate. "You guys barely know each other."

"Eddie. I've been living with him for almost a year. And it wasn't exactly the kind of year that goes easy on a relationship. We're in it for the long haul."

"He was pretty good for you after the surgery," I admit grudgingly. "But marriage? Isn't that all sort of heteronormative?"

"Believe it or not, hets are people too." He snorts. "I really didn't expect you to take this so badly."

"I'm not taking it badly. Give a guy a minute to adjust his worldview."

"Think you can adjust it enough to be my best man?"

"Of course I can. Ben, I really *am* happy for you." I smile at him, and hope it reaches my eyes. "I love you, and I want you to be happy. Congratulations."

"Thank you."

The conversation turns to business, and I've never been so relieved to talk about sales figures and customer-loyalty incentive programs. By the time I walk him to the door, I've gotten over my initial shock, and if I hold him a little too tightly when I hug him good-bye, he's kind enough not to say anything.

After his car rumbles away, I stretch out on my bed and stare at the ceiling for what feels like an hour, hanging with my favorite ghost, What Might Have Been. From the day Ben, an earnest high school freshman, hit on me—the only out gay guy in school, and three years older—his feelings for me had been sweet and uncomplicated—friendship and sometimes lust. Love, but not the kind of love people write songs about. I'm happy for him to find the love he deserves, but it reminds me how lonely I really am. And now I feel like an asshole, making my best friend's engagement news about me. Self-absorbed much, Ed?

My phone ringing jerks me out of my maudlin reveries. I answer on autopilot with a gruff, businesslike "Russell."

"Mr. Russell, this is Amanda at Mercedes-Benz of Lake Lovelace, how are you this evening?" She barely pauses for my answer before she tells me the tire has been replaced and balanced, the alignment checked, and the airbag replaced. "We don't do bodywork in-house, but as a convenience to you, we'd be happy to contract that work to one of our partners."

"Who are the partners?"

"Import Haus or Carver Paint and Body, both are out of town a bit, but have solid reputations and are certified to work on

Mercedes-Benz vehicles. I believe Carver P&B is closer to your home, but Import Haus has been in business longer."

"My brother does that sort of thing . . ."

What the hell. "Take it to Carver, pay whatever he asks. Charge it to the card you all have on file."

"Thank you, Mr. Russell. Is there anything further I can help you with this evening?"

"No, thank you."

Dinner at Keith's. My god, I love the guy, but I don't know if I can handle seeing him and his happy sub tonight. It's been a week since the accident, my car is back in my possession, and my brain seems to be looping a continuous replay of the best sex I've had in years. Seeing the guy I go to for a good beating isn't likely to help me forget Wish. Of course, my mama didn't raise me in a barn, so when Keith texts me to confirm, I dig deep and reply: *What's Heather serving? I'll bring the wine.*

A few moments later, Keith texts back: *Salmon, I think. She liked that Viognier you brought last time.*

Perfect.

When I arrive at Keith's house and he opens the door, Heather is nowhere to be seen and Keith appears troubled. He's a big, handsome guy with pierced ears and a short, well-groomed beard. Although he could pass for midthirties, today he looks every one of his forty-six years, and has a deep groove between his eyebrows. But I can smell food cooking, and there's music playing, so whatever's on his mind likely isn't related to dinner. I hand him the wine and give him a quick hug.

A part of me wants to drop to my knees and beg him to hurt me.

Authority rolls off Keith in waves. Though definitely more of a Dom than a sadist, he's good with masochistic subs. I started going to his club years ago in hopes of scratching an itch sex alone couldn't touch. We've done plenty of scenes, though we've never had sex—he's not gay, but he's talented with a flogger and the things he's done to me with nothing but his voice and a paddle? *Shiver.* Straight girls have all the luck.

"Ed?" He puts a hand on my shoulder. "Are you okay?"

I shake my head to clear my thoughts. "I was going to ask you the same thing. Sorry. Just, damn, sugar, sometimes I wish you were gay. It's been a weird week."

He laughs, holds up the bottle. "I'll bring this to Heather in the kitchen, and I'll ask her to fix you something stronger. Unless . . ." He cocks his head. "Ed, if you need . . ."

"Oh, god, Keith. I can't ask you to—"

"To what? Spank your hot little ass? Clamp your nipples? Slap your cock? Squeeze your balls? Tie you down and make you hurt until it feels good?"

I moan. I want it.

His voice drops low and sexy. "Bend you over my knee and have Heather count the strikes? Send you home still hard with an order not to touch yourself so you can think about what a naughty shit you are? Or maybe I'll let Heather get you off. She loves that, you know. How much it embarrasses you to get off in a woman's hand. It gets her wet."

I'm erect and aching now, and I whimper when he cups my cheek with his palm. "Or maybe I should put your cock in a cage so you can't get it up. Yeah, take full advantage of that sexy piercing of yours. What do you need, Ed? All you have to do is ask. I'm not your Dom, but I *am* your friend. If I can help you, I will."

Shame washes over me, red-hot and tangling like a wet lump in my throat. No matter what I said to Wish about humiliation not being my usual kink, when it *does* work for me, it really, *really* does. I shudder hard, and because he's looking at me expectantly, and because I trust him, I answer.

"I appreciate the offer, but I played with a new sadist the other night—sex too. It was hot, but it was just a one-off. Part of what made it so hot was how much he wanted *me*. So, yeah, I want that, but I would want it to be because you want me, not because you feel sorry for me."

He drops his hand. "Ah, Ed. I'm sorry, buddy. I love playing with you. I like the way you love the pain. But . . ." He glances pointedly toward the kitchen.

"Exactly. It's just pain—for both of us."

"I'll go get you a glass of wine," he says as he walks away, leaving me with my thoughts. I've not always wanted sex with the pain. Self-denial can be a hell of a lot of fun. There've been times in my life when getting off was less important than getting good and hurt. But now, after the scorching night I shared with Wish, I want both.

Keith returns a moment later with two glasses of wine.

"Have you talked to Davis Fox this week?" he asks, handing me a glass.

"Not since the accident, why?"

"Rodney Romeo is making my life miserable."

Oh, that asshole. I fight back the urge I feel to snarl whenever I hear that name. My loathing of him sits heavy on my skin, but this isn't about me now. Shit. No wonder Keith is stressed. Romeo has been hunting for ways to put Keith's BDSM club out of business for years.

"What's he doing this time?"

"He's resurrected the roads bill. I'd have thought you'd be all over that—your dealership: the land would be taken by eminent domain if the bridge proposal goes through."

Fuck me sideways. My dealership. The pro shop. Ben. The cushion against depression and relapse I've spent years carefully cultivating *for Ben.* I sit up straighter.

"They killed that project for lack of funding."

"Romeo wants to bring it back. He thinks he can get the project federal funds, but even if he can't, he's got a nasty tax proposal laid out to pay for it. Sin taxes. Increased taxes on alcohol sales, and on memberships to private clubs which serve alcohol."

"That fucker. How is he going to sell an increase to the country club set?" I know those guys; they aren't going to take kindly to higher taxes—on anything—though they can afford it. Keith's customers are not necessarily rich and powerful, and this could hurt his bottom line, and potentially the viability of the club.

"I don't know, but so far they seem to be supporting him."

Well, *shit.* I hope I don't have to play golf to solve this. I fucking *hate* golf.

"What if I bought in with you? I can help float you so you don't have to pass the costs on to your customers."

"No offense, but Romeo hates me enough already. And after you signed his kid to a sponsorship contract behind his back? Your name on my club would be poison. Come on, Ed. You knew that would come around to bite you."

"Hey, I let the kid out of the contract as soon as Liquid Force showed an interest. Which they wouldn't have done if he hadn't won the tournament. Which wouldn't have happened if he hadn't had a sponsor. I did his kid a favor, and I didn't have to."

"You manipulated a thirteen-year-old kid in a game of 'whose dick is bigger' with his dad, and it doesn't matter if the end result was a good one. You humiliated Romeo in front of thousands of people."

I wave my hand. "You know that's bullshit. No one cared about that. They were pumped to see the hometown kid win."

"Rodney Romeo cared about it. And you and I could both be fucked now."

I hang my head. He's right. I know he's right. But still . . . Ah, fuck.

"I'm sorry, Keith. We'll fix it. I have some pull with the city council, seeing as how my granddaddy built this town. They'll listen if I say widening the bridge is going to 'spoil the small-town feel' of Lake Lovelace."

"Okay. Well, let me know how I can help." He sips his wine. "So, what else is going on?"

"Ben's getting married." I pinch the skin at the bridge of my nose. "I have a lot on my mind." Okay, so maybe Ben isn't the only one on my mind, but his upcoming nuptials are the easiest explanation for why I'm out of sorts. As for that night with Wish—it's starting to feel surreal—it couldn't have been as good as I remember it; I just hadn't had good sex in so long, it's sticking with me.

"Tell him congratulations from me and Heather."

"I will."

"You haven't been to the club in a while. You know, you don't have to play. You could come to hang out."

"Maybe I'll come by sometime this week." Sometimes, sex in the club seems too sanitized, too impersonal. Too tame.

"You know Gabe would love to see you."

"Oh, no. Keith. I can't. The last time was so disappointing."

"I thought you liked hairy old bears?"

"Sugar, he was adorable. And he knew his knots. He was amazing right up until he had me all tied up and then was afraid to put any muscle into it when he hit me." The utter disappointment of that night washes over me. "Seriously, Keith, you have the worst taste in men."

Keith laughs. "He's a nice guy, and he thought you were cute. He didn't want to hurt you."

"Story of my fucking life." I grunt. "And a waste of beautiful bondage."

"For Gabe, the bondage was the main event. You know, he might have put more effort into the flogging if you hadn't answered the phone in the middle of it."

"It was Ben." I shrug. "I don't let Ben's calls go to voice mail. Ever."

Keith sighs. "I know, and I understand why, but you do realize he has Davis now. He doesn't . . ."

"Don't finish that sentence, please."

"Dinner's ready," Heather announces from the doorway. Saved by the bell.

chapter FOUR

the club smells like leather, and a little like sweat. The bouncer waves me through, his bored expression turning to an appreciative leer as I walk past. Once inside, I take in the view in front of me. It's quiet—subdued—tonight. The main dance floor is mostly empty, though a couple sways absently to the beat in the corner.

"Ed?" I hear Keith behind me, and he sounds surprised. Hadn't I said I'd come by this week? I turn, jutting my chin just *so*, hopeful he might be up for playing tonight.

"Hello, sugar. Did you miss me?"

He grins. "It's been three days, not three years. But I love seeing you here. Are you with someone?"

"Nope."

"There's someone I'd like you to meet."

"I thought we covered the fact that you have the worst taste in men."

Keith laughs. "All right. Too bad, I think you'd like Wish."

Wish. Here. After my initial shock—of course, why wouldn't he seek out Keith's club after I mentioned it?—the name sends a rush of longing through me. But my reasons for not dating him are still valid. I glance around, but I don't see him. Maybe he's playing with someone in one of the private rooms. I try to ignore the sharp pang of jealousy at that thought.

". . . watched him with the subs; he's pretty intense. Only plays with men. Heather says he's really handsome."

"I'm sure he's lovely, but the only wish that's going to be in my pants tonight is this one." I grab my dick and give it a squeeze.

He reaches down and cups my cock. It's been a little plump since I came in—the smell of the place is enough to give me a hopeful semi, but when Keith squeezes me, I harden in his hand. His grip tightens before he lets go, then he flicks my fly with his thumb, hitting my piercing through the zipper. It's a sharp nip of pain, and the shock of it makes my eyes roll back in delight.

"Oh, sugar." I shudder. "Got any more of that for me?"

I can tell the moment he decides he's in. His lips twist—it's an intimate tell, something only someone who knows him would notice. He's going to make me work for it.

"Heather is sick," he murmurs. "It's hotter when she's here to watch."

"That's what you get for fucking breeding, Keith. They go off to school and bring back the plague." I roll my eyes for effect. He wants me to pick a fight; I'll give him a fucking reason to hit me.

The slap comes without warning, across my face, open hand, a sharp *crack*. The bouncer's head snaps up, but then he sees it's Keith and me and he knows the game. There's a whole lot of *not my kink* in this world, but yeah, an openhanded slap across the face is *so* my kink. And Keith's employees know it.

"Watch your mouth, Ed," Keith growls low.

"Make me," I growl back, and it's *on*. He grabs my hair in his fist and drags me across the room. He walks fast, pulling me off-balance as I stumble after him, following the pain and him wherever they'll take me.

A bench. He pushes me against it, hard, and lets go of my hair. He kicks my feet apart and shoves me down so my face hits the wood, my ass in the air. A tumble of laughter spills out of me. It's absolutely delightful to be thrown around like this. Like he fucking means it.

"That's it? Hair pulling? No wonder your wife stayed home," I taunt. "I bet she's not even sick. Unless boredom is a disease now."

Crack. An openhanded swat across my backside. It would be better if I were naked. I reach for my belt, but he slaps my hand away.

"Put your hands back on the bench," Keith orders. "And shut the fuck up about my *submissive*."

He ties my hands, then my legs at the ankles. God, I'm so hard now. I'm not going to get fucked tonight, but at this point I don't even care. He's going to hit me. Not a playful slap on the mouth or swat on the ass, he's going to fucking hurt me.

He pulls a hood over my face. Not a blindfold, but a hood. I shudder. I don't like the hood. I've never liked the hood.

"Asshole," I snarl at him.

"You don't like the hood," he grits through his teeth, "you can use your fucking safeword."

"Fuck. You."

"That's what I thought."

Inside the blackness of the hood, unease creeps into me. I hate not being able to see, and I hate feeling the fabric on my ears. The apprehension will make it harder for me to relax into the scene, and Keith knows it. He's always been good at knowing exactly how to push me out of my comfort zone to make everything more intense.

He steps up close behind me and reaches around my waist to undo my belt. With a rough tug, he pulls my pants down to expose me. Freed from the confines of my jeans, my dick slaps against the wooden bench.

"You forgot to take off my shirt. Are you sure you've done this before?"

"I'm not going to flog you."

"Asshole," I snarl again. This time, the flick of his thumb hits my guiche piercing, back behind my balls, and a tight spasm washes through me.

"We have an audience. Maybe I'll let him join in." Keith gives the ring another flick, then runs a soothing hand down my side. When he speaks again, it's directed out, away from me. "Hi, Wish."

I shudder, off-balance, turned-on, and self-conscious all at once.

"I didn't know you played with men, Keith."

Wish's voice is bright with surprise.

"I don't know why I bother with this one." Keith steps away from me, cold air where his body heat had been warming me. "Except the little slut likes pain, and I fucking love hurting him."

"May I watch?" His voice sounds almost bored now, but I can tell he wants this. Does he know it's me yet? Does he recognize my body? I'm still mostly clothed.

"That's fine," Keith tells him.

My safeword pops into my head; I don't know why. I usually get off on being watched, and this is Wish, the guy who fucked me senseless and then cuddled me all night. I try to shrug it away, end up literally shrugging, and it turns into a shudder of anticipation. I want him to watch, and I want him angry.

"No," I whisper.

"What's that, Ed?" Keith leans close to my hooded face.

"No, I don't want him to watch." I flush red when I say the lie, not that anyone can see with the hood over my face. By now, Wish knows it's me. Will he play my game, or will he walk away?

"Tough shit. You come into my place of business and start mouthing off about my wife and kids? I want everybody to watch me stripe your skinny ass for that."

"You're going to cane him?" Wish's voice isn't disinterested anymore. And damn it, now that I know what's coming . . . a caning is hard to take, even for me, and Keith knows it. He's going to break me down in front of . . . in front of Wish. He's not just going to hurt me, he's going to humiliate me too.

Keith's answer comes in the first blow. The cane whistles through the air slightly before it connects with the back of my thighs. A tight, hot pain—a warning crack.

"Count." The order comes from Wish, not Keith, but my response is automatic.

"One."

The next strike hits my ass, just across the fleshiest part. Not hard enough.

"Two."

The third blow has more force behind it and hits right over the thinnest part of my ass. This sensation is darker—there's bone involved. I flinch away, which drags my cock across the bench, my Prince Albert catching on the edge and sending blinding pain behind my eyes.

"Fuck." I try to breathe through it, try to find some center of control.

"Three," Wish corrects me. "Say it."

"Th-three," I grind out. The fourth stroke hits the exact same spot and I can't help it, I shout. "Four!"

And then I start to cry. A little gasp, not even a sob, but it rushes out of me at the same time the cane strikes the back of my thighs again.

"Fi-hive."

A sixth blow follows quickly and tears are flowing freely inside the blackness of the hood.

"Count," Wish orders, and I shake my head. "Count."

"Can't." I whimper. If I count, the caning will resume. I want it, I want it desperately, but I still can't make myself say the number. I groan into the bench.

"Then Wish will count them for you." Keith runs a fingertip over one of the cane marks, and the sensation makes me arch with shivery bliss.

"Six."

Seven tears a real sob out of me.

Eight makes me safeword.

"Yellow," I gasp.

"Ed?" Keith's voice is calm, familiar. "You okay, buddy?"

I shake my head. "I hate the fucking hood. I hate the fucking cane. I hate you."

Lies, but in the moment it feels true.

"Do you want to stop? Take off the hood?"

Do I?

"Yes." I nod.

He pulls the hood off me. "Do you want me to untie you?"

I shake my head, eyes still closed because I'm not ready to see Wish. Grateful the hood is gone.

"Do you want me to hit you again?"

"I want . . . something else. Not the cane."

"I'm going to untie you, Ed."

"No!" Panic grips me. If he unties me, there's a chance I could turn around and punch him. I'm all adrenaline and frustration right now, sexual and otherwise. I *need* something.

"Do you want me to leave?" Wish asks, addressing me directly. He's moved around to the other side of the bench, standing in front of me. Leaning close? I open my eyes. No, not leaning; he's squatting so we're eye-to-eye. My hard-hat-wearing angel, hair flopping on his forehead and half covering bright-blue eyes. He lifts a hand like he wants to touch my face.

"It's okay," I tell him. "You can stay."

"Can I touch you?" He asks me, not Keith. I nod slowly, captivated by his calm gaze. He slides a hand along the side of my face, cups the back of my neck, and strokes. "You're okay now, yeah?"

"Yeah."

"Good." He smiles his gorgeous, slightly crooked, smile. His hand tightens. "I'd like to play with you some, if you're up for it?"

Am I? My erection flagged during the caning, but I'm still aroused, still *wanting*. And maybe that's all it is—maybe pain without sex wasn't enough for me tonight, in spite of my intentions.

I glance over my shoulder at Keith, who seems to be admiring the marks on my ass as he rubs them softly. I'd been so focused on Wish, I'd forgotten about Keith.

"Keith? Do you mind?"

Keith smiles. "I told you, I thought you'd like him. Have fun. I can step back and supervise if you want me to."

"Thanks, sugar, but that won't be necessary." I turn back to Wish. "Untie me, we should talk."

He releases the cuffs, helps me stand upright. I step out of my shoes and jeans, scoop them up to take with me. My ass and thighs throb. Glancing around, I see the closest booth is empty. I gesture toward it with my chin, and he follows me. When I sit, pain radiates from my ass to hallelujah and I shiver. I pull myself together: a jut of my chin, a tone to my voice. *Armor.*

"Are you going to tell me why you safeworded?"

"I thought we could say hello first." I smile at him. "Catch up?"

"I thought it was a hookup." His voice is flat.

I casually shrug. "Easier, you know."

"For who?" He glares at me. Oooh, that gets my blood flowing. I drop my hand to my lap and give my dick a squeeze.

"Stop that." He slaps my hand away from my cock. "We're talking first." There's a bit of mockery in his voice now. "Why did you safeword? Was it the cane?"

"The cane was fine. I was out of sorts for other reasons."

"The hood?"

"I don't like having my head covered like that. Not ever. I don't even like to wear hats. Keith knows I hate it, but we were—"

"I saw. The role play. Riling him up, calling him a breeder, and insulting his bedroom skills. Was the fact that I was watching part of it? You told him no but you didn't safeword. I assumed you weren't really protesting."

"I wasn't really protesting, but yeah, it was part of it. The sight deprivation, it made me uneasy. And I wanted to rile you up a little too. Conflict turns me on."

"But you're okay with playing with me now?"

I study him carefully. "Why do you want to play with me after how I treated you?"

"I'm twenty-four years old; I'm not going to apologize for what gets me off," he says in a lilting impression of my voice. Okay, there's a point for him. He glances over to the bench. "Keith threw you down over there. You laughed, and it was like you'd started living in that moment. Watching you come alive like that made my dick so goddamned hard. Watching you take a caning—and he was really pushing you—that was intense."

He drops his gaze to his hands, then smiles again. "Why do I want to play with you? Because you turn me on. I want to hit you. I want to fuck you. I don't want to own you or master you or any of that Dom shit. I'm not looking for a waxed body to push around and call mine. I want to watch a grown man take a goddamned beating and thrive on it."

Holy fuck. Wrap me in paper and stick a bow on me because I am sold.

"Come here." I pat the couch next to me, and he scoots closer, placing a hand on my thigh. It feels good, warm and friendly, and his pinkie finger strokes me gently, almost absently. My heart starts racing as I remember our night together the week before—but it isn't the orgasms or the sex or even the pain that runs through my head as my dick starts plumping up. It's the way he held me while I drank the tea, and the way he kissed me like he was praying for something.

"I sent my car to your brother. For the bodywork," I blurt out, not even sure why.

His lips quirk in a smile and I see a flash of teeth. "I know." He squeezes my leg. "I helped work on it."

My mouth drops open, and he laughs.

"Why so shocked, S-Class? I'm sure I'm not the only guy you've ever dated who works more than one job."

"We're not—" I start to correct him, but then he's kissing me, and I can't remember why anything else matters.

He nibbles at my lower lip and buries a hand in my hair, clutching at it like a lifeline as he takes my mouth. I reach, needing to feel skin under my palms, and I jerk up on his T-shirt until I get my hands underneath it, run my palms over that flat stomach and give in to the need to explore, to give a pleasure that's about sex, yes, but about more than that. This fan-fucking-tastic connection between us.

The hand on my thigh reaches around to my burning ass and grips hard enough to make me squirm from the pain still throbbing under the cane marks. He breaks the kiss to whisper in my ear, "These are so fucking hot. Want to fuck you while you wriggle like this."

His fingertips dig in along one of the welts, and I go shivery in my belly, wanting to give him that, wanting to make up for being a cranky old queen when all he's ever been was nice to me. But more than anything—wanting to be alone with him.

"Let's go to my place," I murmur as he bites my earlobe.

He pulls back and stares at me a moment. "If it's a hookup, I'd just as soon stay here."

Oh, he really doesn't play fair, does he? I search his face for some indication that he'll change his mind, that I can talk him into coming home with me without giving anything away besides my very eager ass, but his expression is all challenge and unmovable calm.

"You're . . ."

"Twenty-four years old. A grown-up, last I checked. I rent a decent place, I have a steady job, and I even have a cat."

"Baby, I don't want to know about your pussy." I try for levity, but his smile doesn't reach his eyes.

"I like you, Eddie S-Class. And yeah, I wanna fuck you. But I don't appreciate being treated like the help."

"The hel—? I did not." Outrage makes me snarl, but he doesn't back down.

"Get off and get out is not my scene. I told you what I wanted. Now we're both here, by some coincidence, because we wanted to get off. And with any one of those little pain-sluts out there—" he gestures toward the rest of the club "—I'd be all over that. But that's not what I want from you."

He stares me down. I can't remember the last time someone stared me down.

"What—exactly—do you want, lovely? I don't agree to anything without knowing the terms."

"Always a business man, aren't you? I want sex—as much of it as we can have. And I want to get to know the guy I'm sleeping with." A shrug. "I'm a simple man, S-Class."

"I'm not." The words burst out of me before I can stop them. I blush, and despite the closeness of his body and the intimacy of the club, I shiver, and goose bumps peak across my skin.

"I know." He pulls me closer, running his big palms over my naked thighs and ass to warm them. "I don't need to know all your secrets. Just, I dunno, how you drink your coffee and what you like on your pizza. The things you get to know about a guy you're seeing."

"Black. And cheese."

"See, that's a start. And you prefer ham to avocado in your sandwiches, and you drink hibiscus tea."

"Yeah," I agree, fatigue starting to press in on me. "The buzz from the caning is wearing off, and I'm getting . . ."

"Stand up." He helps me to my feet, and the next thing I know, he's sliding my pants over my legs and helping me slip into my shoes. "Did you drive?"

I shake my head. "No, never here. If I play, I'm too wrung out afterward to drive."

He frowns. "I took a cab myself."

"So we'll take another cab back to my place." I shrug, then smile. "I'll let you look at the pictures on my walls. I might even tell you about the people in them. But you have to promise to fuck me hard first."

"Deal."

When we get into the cab, he pulls me practically into his lap. The welts on my ass burn in protest at being dragged across the seat, but I don't care. Sometimes the souvenirs are even better than the beating itself. Squirming to chase that sensation a little more, I lean into him and kiss him, slow and deep, wrapping my arms around his neck and rubbing us together, chest to chest.

"God, I love this," he whispers against my lips. "I could kiss you all night."

Oh yeah, I could definitely be on board with that plan. I scoot even closer, throwing one leg across his lap so I can grind my hardening cock into his thigh. His hands sneak up under my shirt without any apparent destination, simply petting me, letting me feel the cool blast of air conditioning in contrast to the warmth of his palms.

I feel like a horny teenager, rutting in the backseat of the car, one hand on his chest, the other clutching the sizeable bulge in his pants. He slides a hand down the back of mine and squeezes, sending little starbursts of pain through me and making me squirm.

I lose myself in his kiss, let myself fly on the sensations of pain and arousal twining together. The gentleness of his hands on my ass sets a slow rhythm between us, as inevitable as waves lapping on the shore. By the time the cab pulls up in front of my house and I shove a handful of bills at the driver, I'm so turned on I can barely breathe— from kissing! We stumble from the cab to the house, still groping each other, and somehow I manage to get us inside without dropping my keys.

Wish shoves me up against the front door, wrapping his arms around my waist. I love that he's the same height as me, that we can stare right into each other's eyes while he tells me, "I want you, Eddie S-Class. You make me crazy with it. Can't wait to get you naked, see every bit of your sexy skin. Want to leave marks on you you'll feel for days. Want to make you cry. Want to make you come so hard you never forget me."

I don't tell him he's already unforgettable. That ego of his doesn't need any more stroking. I pull my clothes off and I'm reaching for his. He stops me, pushing my hand away.

"Shoes first," he whispers.

Oh, hell.

I'm not a submissive. I don't get turned on by following orders, and I sure-as-the-orgasm-he-promised-me don't have a kink for being on my knees. But I want him naked, and the shoes do have to come off. I glare at him, and he stares back—how the fuck is he so calm?

"So take them off," I growl.

"It doesn't make you weak, taking care of another person."

"I know that."

"So why won't you take off my shoes?"

"Why do you want me on my knees?" I counter. "I thought you weren't into that Dom shit."

"Why is your dick so fucking hard?" He slides his fingers down my shaft, cups my balls, and flicks behind them, hitting the ring back there with perfect accuracy.

I drop to my knees.

My face flushes with anger and resentment as I slip his feet from his shoes and roll his socks off. I thrust them aside and start to stand, but his hand, rough on my shoulder, holds me down. I scowl at his bare feet, seething with a frustration I can't put into words. What gives this man the right to make me speechless?

He lets go of my shoulder, snatches my hair, and jerks my head up without warning.

"Fuck!" I shout, jumping to my feet. "What the fuck is wrong with you?"

He throws me back against the door, his hand still in my hair the only thing keeping me from bouncing right off the hard wood surface. Ah, *fuck yeah.*

We struggle for a moment, pushing, wrestling, grappling for advantage. A thrill shoots through me like electricity as I get a good grip on him. I haul him around by his clothes, shove him backward, and slam him against the entryway wall with a loud *thunk.*

He tosses his head back and laughs, then lunges for me again. This time, he gets a hand around my wrist and twists my arm behind me. I swing with my other arm, which he plucks from the air like he's catching a ball, and I'm well and truly caught.

Arousal makes my limbs heavy, a rich warmth spreading through me. My heart races with the rush of the tussle, and I squirm against him one last time, grateful to feel his hard cock through his pants. The best part of wrestling with a lover is the point of acquiescence, that moment of being overpowered and knowing I'm going to get fucked.

"God*damn,* S-Class," he whispers. "I want you so fucking bad. I had plans, you know? I was going to spank you until your ass was red all over. I wanted to dig my fingers into the stripes on your ass until you screamed. Now all I can think of is getting inside you."

Oh, god. He *is* inside me. He's got me figured out better than any lover has in my whole life. He's under my skin and in my head, and I want nothing more than to take him inside my body and rut.

"Do you have a fucking condom?" I growl, my hands clenching in his grip behind my back.

"If I reach for it, will you stay put?"

"Yes."

He lets go of my wrists, and there's a rustle of fabric as he strips off his clothes, and then the crinkle of foil. "It's lubricated, is that enough for you?"

I nod, letting him maneuver me, the side of my face pressing into the intricate carving in the door's mahogany surface.

It's not enough lube, the little amount on a condom never is, but the burn of pain as he pushes inside me makes me groan out helplessly. He lets go of my wrists again and grips my ass, sending a current of dull pain through me when his fingers dig into the welts from the caning.

I have to brace myself against the door with my hands as he fucks me hard. He spits into his palm and uses it to jerk me roughly, taking me right up to the edge. I'm wild and alive and so turned on I could scream, need and heat and lust sharpening my senses.

His lips skim my shoulder, gentle and sweet, and the shocking contrast between that touch and the relentless fucking is what tips me over. I lay my head back against him and trust him to hold me up, my limbs shaking as I roar with the release, my body lit up like Christmas in his arms.

He does hold me up, and he doesn't stop fucking me through it, so strong he can support my weight and drive me into the door at the same time. When he comes, he shouts out my name in a strangled plea for god-knows-what.

We sink to the stone-tiled floor, gasping for breath, our hands clutching at each other in a helpless, instinctual search for closeness. We find our fit: my head on his chest, one of his hands tangled in my hair. The slow descent back to sanity is marked by the heaving of our chests, and my soft laughter—the laughter of the truly well-fucked.

"What's so funny?" he asks, his own voice tinged with humor.

"That's me appreciating your prowess," I mumble against his chest. "Holy everything, that was good."

He slaps my ass playfully. "Yeah it was."

"Let's do it again." I kiss his nipple and it tightens against my lips.

"In the morning," he says, his voice firm. "I'm only human, S-Class."

"You called me Eddie when we were fucking." I feel somewhat stung by his return to the nickname after what we shared.

"Yeah." He kisses the side of my head. "Eddie." It sounds so sweet like that, in his hushed postcoital tone. "Can I sleep in that big, warm bed of yours and beat your ass in the morning, Eddie?"

Fuck, yes.

"I'll take it as a personal insult if you don't." I yawn, stretching alongside him.

"I promise to only insult you *before* sex." Chuckling, he stands and ducks into the powder room, I assume to dispose of the condom. When he returns, he hauls me to my feet. "Bedtime, babe. I feel an overwhelming desire to cuddle you senseless."

I laugh and follow him up the stairs to my bedroom, where I let him do just that.

chapter FIVE

Wish sleeps in on weekends. His body curls around mine; our legs tangle together. It's a much nicer way to wake up than to someone doing yoga at the foot of my bed. I roll and stretch, loving the rub of the sheet against my bruised body. We'd woken twice in the night to fuck, and the second time, Wish held me down and slapped my ass until it burned like a witch at the stake. Goddamn, that feels amazing now.

His eyes flutter open, and he smiles at me, so handsome and sleepy, it makes me wish I were a photographer so I could capture that veiled promise.

"C'mere, S-Class," he growls, pulling my groin flush to his. I wrap my arms around his neck and indulge in some serious morning making out. He kisses me deep and slow, like he wants it to last, but our hips rocking together and his hands on my nipples hurry us right along until I'm panting, holding back my orgasm by sheer force of will.

"Eddie? What the hell, man?"

Ben's voice from behind me is like a bucket of ice water dumped on the bed. I stop rutting against my fine new friend and roll to face my confused best friend.

"Darling, if you're going to burst into my boudoir on a Saturday morning and interrupt the proceedings, have the decency to do so naked." I glare at him and raise a pointed eyebrow at his board shorts. He blushes to the roots of his hair, but he glares back.

Board shorts. I glance at the date on my watch and sink back down onto the bed, a blush of my own stealing up my face. "I forgot, didn't I?"

"Ya think?" he growls. "Dave has the Nautique tied up to your dock, Ridley is doing something probably illegal as fuck on a jet ski in front of your neighbor's house, and I just came in here to help you load your shit into the boat. I wasn't expecting to interrupt Kinky Eddie's youth outreach program!"

"Hey, asshole." Wish sits up in bed and he looks mad enough to spit, his face turning red. "Show some fucking manners and go wait outside."

To my utter shock, Ben shuts his mouth and backs out of the room, closing the door behind him.

"Please tell me that is not your boyfriend." Wish pinches the skin at the top of his nose and peeks at me from between his fingers.

"Worse." I collapse against the pillows with a *thump*. "*That* is my best friend, Ben. And he's having a thing today, spending the day on the lake with family and friends, to celebrate being sober for nine years. And I forgot because . . ." I gesture between us, letting the words hang in the air.

"Dude." Wish slumps beside me.

"I know." I bury my face against his shoulder. "He's not really an asshole, you know."

He runs a hand through my hair. It makes me want to snuggle closer. "He probably wouldn't be your best friend if he was. I was hoping to spend the day with you."

The day, the weekend, as much time naked as we could manage, it all sounds wonderful. But Ben . . . "He's family. You know how it is with family."

He smiles at me then. "Yeah, family is important. Kinda weird meeting them when they barge into the bedroom in the middle of sex though."

I can't help it, I laugh. "Awk-ward."

He laughs too, a funny, snorty laugh that suits him perfectly, but then he asks in this tiny, hopeful voice, "Can I come?"

I sit up straight. "You want to, really?"

"I want to hang out with you." He shows a flash of teeth. "And if you're celebrating Big Ben's sobriety, I am too."

A little piece of me I didn't even realize was frozen melts under the force of that.

"Yeah, lovely. You can come. Want to borrow a bathing suit?"

I'm not one to brag—okay, that's a lie, I love to brag—but my date looks amazing in a Speedo. When Wish comes out of the en suite with his bulge on full display in teensy orange trunks, it's all I can do not to wrestle him down to the bed and keep him there for a week. But Ben's outside, and the rest of my little family is waiting for us, so I leer a bit instead.

"I cannot believe you wear these." He gives my ass a once-over. "And have them in a variety of colors. You know your thighs are still striped. Everyone will be able to see them."

I can't help smirking. "That's the intent, isn't it? What's the point of being an exhibitionist if you don't, you know, *exhibit*?"

He shakes his head in this completely adorable he-wishes-he-were-exasperated-but-he-just-can't way. "Come here."

His hands on the sides of my face are a revelation. Their gentleness as they whisper over my cheekbones has me rolling my face into his palms like a kitten, eyes closed, chest heaving. He kisses me with no-holds-barred, a lush, sensual attack of lips and tongue that turns me on and on.

Then he pulls back, smiling, and whispers, "Now you're definitely exhibiting."

I glance down at our matching hard-ons in fancy swimwear and snort a laugh. "Oh, you are something else, lovely. Let's go, I'll introduce you to the fam.'"

"So, who all is going to be there?"

A glance out the window shows Ben in the bow of the wake boat, gesturing at the house and shaking his head while Davis smiles indulgently. Farther down the cove, the plume of water from Ridley's jet ski arcs into the air in stop-and-go figure eights. I start ticking the crew off on my fingers as we head down the stairs.

"Ben and his fiancé, Davis. Davis's kid brother, Ridley—and I do mean kid; he's fourteen. Tina and Elvis for sure."

"Elvis?"

"Tina's dog. He's one of those so-ugly-he's-cute critters. She brings him everywhere. Ben's folks probably didn't come down from Georgia, but I'm sure he invited them."

"So how do you know Ben?"

"We've been friends since high school—and he works for me. He was a professional wakeboarder. Now he's retired and he runs a pro shop out of my boat dealership."

In the kitchen, I start throwing Cokes and bottled water into a cooler, and I give the coffee machine a longing glance. Ben will have energy drinks on the boat, but it really isn't the same.

"He does this every year?"

I shrug. "Some years he feels more celebratory than others." Like years when he gets engaged versus years when he's having a big fight with his boyfriend and facing possibly life-destroying surgery. Last year, nobody dared even bring up the idea of a celebration. We were all focused on keeping him too busy to wallow. "One of the reasons this is a big deal: He had spinal surgery last fall—he'd been putting it off for years. So it's more than his sobriety, you know?"

Wish nods. "Yeah. I get it."

Cooler full, I dump the contents of my ice maker in it, and we head out the back door, across the perfectly manicured lawn and down the dock to Dave's waiting boat.

"About time, Ed." Dave stands up and reaches for the cooler. I hand it over and step into the boat.

I feel Wish step behind me, bracing himself on the wake tower with one hand, and wrapping the other around my waist. No time like the present to make this introduction.

"Ben, Dave, this is Aloysius Carver. My date, darlings." My face heats up, and I notice Ben is blushing too. Dave, usually the blushy one, only grins. I've always suspected Davis has a voyeuristic streak, but Ben won't confirm or deny.

"Nice to meet you, Aloysius." Dave sticks out a hand.

"Call me Wish."

The niceties are repeated, and then, finally, we can get on our way. I stretch out as best I can on the boat, letting the hot vinyl and the sun warm my skin. The scents of sweat and sunscreen and Ben's energy drink roll over me and the muscles in my body start to relax, giving up their tension to the lake and the sunshine and that special magic the combination works on my soul. I close my eyes and breathe it all in. God, I love the lake.

"Are we picking up Tina?" I tilt my head toward Ben and open one eye.

"No." Ben frowns. "Her washing machine flooded her kitchen. She's waiting for the repair guy, said she'd call around noon."

Ugh, what a way to ruin a Saturday. "She's still coming, right?"

"Said she wouldn't miss it." Ben flashes his megawatt grin.

Ridley pulls up alongside the boat to wave hello and then goes back behind us, jumping wakes and hooting and hollering and in general clowning around. It makes me smile. I grew up on this lake, same as Ridley, and I feel a weird kinship with him. Even if his world is markedly different than mine was thirty years ago, we're both a product of this town in a way even his brother and Ben are not. Lake Lovelace is our home and our legacy. My grandfather and his great grandfather had both been among the group of developers who created the lake and founded the town around it. I wonder if he feels the same responsibility toward it that was nurtured in me.

Ben and Dave's house is tucked away on a little cove—it's not great for wakeboarding, but it's mostly deserted, so it's a great place to hang out. Ridley and his friends have built a long rail along the side of the cove, and one of them is sliding along it on a wake skate. We slow to a stop and watch as he attempts to dismount and crashes, his skate flying out in the opposite direction.

Ridley whoops and hollers, "Sick slide, Cade!"

"I can't believe they built a rail there." I shake my head. "I can't believe you let them. Aren't they loud as hell all the time?"

Dave shrugs. "He's not loud, he's my brother?" he offers, and yeah, I get it. I don't have siblings of my own—I'm such a cliché, the spoiled only child of wealthy parents—but I know a few people on this planet I'd do anything for, and most of them are sitting in this boat.

Ben lounges in the driver's seat and studies Wish. "You ride?"

Wish shakes his head and puffs out his chest a little. "Willing to give it a try though. Might be fun."

Oh, dear.

Ben bristles at the suggestion that his beloved sport might be anything less than the best fucking thing since actual fucking. To someone who didn't know him, it wouldn't show. No, he's still got that big, amiable grin on his face, and his eyes are hidden behind mirrored shades, but I can tell it's there.

Macho posturing. *So* my kink.

"You can wear Dave's vest. Mine's probably too big for you. Newbie up first." Ben reaches under a seat and digs out the vest, then hands it to him. "What size shoes do you wear?" He glances down at Wish's feet. "Nines?"

"Ten and a half."

"Oh, baby. Be nice." Dave sits down behind Ben and drapes an arm over his shoulder. "I know you're grumpy 'cause you can't ride yet, but don't pick on Eddie's boyfriend. It makes you look jealous."

"I ain't jealous." Ben folds his arms across his chest. "Eddie and I aren't like that."

"Right." Dave rolls his eyes and winks at me. "And Eddie never once told me if I hurt you again, he'd 'rip my spleen out my piss slit with an ice cream scoop.'"

Ben lifts his sunglasses and meets my eyes. "You did that?"

I shrug. "I might have."

Ben snorts. "Surprise, surprise. And why is it always the spleen? All right everyone, no more hazing the newbie." As if the rest of us had been doing any such thing. He turns to Wish. "My bindings will fit you, you can ride my board."

Wish takes to wakeboarding like a fish to water. It seems Ben barely has time to get wet before he's got Wish up on the board. He's strong, he's young, and he's apparently fearless. When Ben finds out Wish used to get annual lift tickets to go snowboarding in Minnesota, they're immediately "bros" even though Ben has seen snow about three times in his whole life. The talk gets technical, occasionally punctuated by a whoop or a yell toward the boat carrying Ridley and his friends.

While Ben and Wish go over the process of turning into a backside slide, Dave plops himself down next to me and hands me an energy drink. "So. You two are what, dating?"

"Nothing so simple as that."

"He do that to you?" Dave gestures to the bruise curling up the side of my thigh. Keith hadn't been holding back on that one. Hell, on any of them if the delicious ache all over my ass and thighs is any indication.

"No, Bedhead, he just watched. Then he took me home, pinned me to the wall, and fucked me hard."

"And you like that?"

There's no judgment in Dave's voice, only a simple curiosity.

"I fucking love it. The adrenaline when I'm itching for a fight, the endorphins when I get tied down and hit, the feeling of being overpowered? I *love* that. It's better than anything."

Dave nods, then glances back to the swim platform, where Ben is miming snowboarding to prove some point. "I can see why you and Ben never . . ."

I grin. "Ben couldn't swat a bee if it stung him."

"Yeah. But if it stung me?"

I bump his shoulder with mine. "Marriage, eh?"

"Yeah. Marriage." His smile turns dazzling.

"Congratulations."

"You know, Ed, it would mean a lot to Ben for you to say that to him. And mean it."

A bark from the end of the dock catches our attention before I can answer. Tina waves, gear bag at her feet and Elvis's rhinestone-covered leash in hand. You expect a purebred purse dog to wear a leash like that, not a forty-pound mutt of indeterminate pedigree. But that's Tina for you—making sure her pet has as much flair as his namesake. In addition to his sparkly leash and collar, he's wearing a life jacket with handles on it. Personally, I suspect Elvis would learn to fly before he'd let her put him in the water, life jacket or no.

"Everybody hold on," I instruct Ben and Wish, who sit down on the sundeck while I putter the boat around to the dock to collect the latest additions to the party.

"Hey, baby." Tina hands Ben the protesting dog and smacks a kiss on his cheek. As soon as Ben sets him down, Elvis scurries under the steering wheel and curls up in a ball.

"Hey, T." Dave holds out his hand to help her onto the boat where she sits down on the sundeck to join the conversation about the similarities in snowboarding and wakeboarding, her husky laugh filling the boat when Wish says something doubtlessly charming.

I nudge Elvis with my toe—I never met a dog who was scared of water before this one. "Okay, buddy?"

He shivers. Looking around me and seeing how well Wish fits in with my little homemade family, I think I have a pretty good idea how he feels.

"Hey Eddie, I'm gonna demonstrate the backside slide for Wish. Give me a pull?" Tina calls out, zipping up her vest.

After Tina rides, Wish takes the rope again, and Dave drives so I can watch while Ben and Tina call out instructions between pulls.

He amazes me—not only trying the slide, but also making a few small jumps and surface turns. Each time, he shouts his triumph and pumps a fist in the air. I'm giddy, watching him. It's so like those early years on the lake with Ben and Tina, nostalgia stings behind my nose. Tina glances up at me and winks, like she's thinking the same thing.

"He's good," she says.

"So were you—that demonstration you did was sick." And she's fit like I haven't seen her in years—not since she quit riding pro. "And you look awesome. You do crunches in your sleep or something?"

She laughs. "The core is a very important muscle group. You'd have a six-pack too if you did some weights to go with your cardio."

"Jocks." I shake my head. "You're all the same."

She laughs again and turns back to watch my date attempt to fly.

When Wish finally sits down next to me, dripping wet and grinning like a kid at Christmas, I can't help myself: I wrap my arms around him and kiss him. I kiss him, not because I've got an exhibitionist streak, but because he's happy, and smiling, and not kissing him when he looks that good would be a crime. He tastes like sunscreen and lake water and joy. *Sweet.*

"Hey, S-Class," he whispers when he breaks away. "I like your family."

"Hey, Hard Hat." I kiss his nose. "I think they like you too."

When we're all hungry and sunburned, the party moves up to the backyard, with Dave and Ben cooking at the grill: brats and burgers and vegetables on skewers. Ridley's buddies take over the swimming pool, and some of Ben and Dave's neighbors come join the crowd. The atmosphere is festive, and when someone puts on music, Wish pulls me into a slow, grinding dance.

"You were amazing out there." I drape my arms over his shoulders. "Like you were born on the lake."

He shrugs, but he looks pleased by the compliment. "It's not so different from snowboarding. Softer landings too. Hey, how come you didn't ride?"

"Because Ben can't. Remember how I said he had surgery last fall? Well, he can't ride for a few more months."

Wish stops dancing and stares at me, hands stilling where they'd been stroking my lower back in languid circles. "So you don't do something you enjoy . . . because he can't. Like not drinking because he's sober."

"I'm supportive." *And defensive.*

"No need to get your back up, man. I get it. He's your friend; you want to help him out. It just seems a little overboard to me. I mean, has he ever actually asked you to deprive yourself for him?"

"No," I admit. "But when you care about someone, you want to do what's best for them, right?"

"Sure, I guess." He glances up at Ben and then back at me. "Yeah, I get it."

He starts us swaying to the music again, and I rest my head on his shoulder. It feels nice, not sexual really, though the chemistry is always there between us. I like the way he smells, a little like sunscreen, a little like the lake, and underneath it, the vestiges of some fragrance no man over thirty would be caught wearing. I nip the side of his throat, and he rumbles appreciatively, palming my ass with one hand. The frisson that runs through me when his fingers dig into the cane marks makes me shudder and realize I don't want to share this moment with anyone but him.

"You want to get out of here?" I ask, breathless.

"What did you have in mind?"

"Home. Takeout. A movie. Bed and some really sweaty sex; the kind where the sheets stick to our skin and the whole room smells like us."

His eyes widen, and he grinds his cock against mine. "Yeah. Um, maybe not in that order?"

I laugh. *Twenty-four.* "Anticipation is good for you."

"Blue balls are not."

"Horn dog."

"Pervert."

Clearly, a match made in heaven.

On Sunday afternoon, I have to take him home, and I'm reluctant for reasons I don't fully understand. I think about picking a fight with him in the car. It would end things fast, or it would end up with us in bed. But I can't do it. I had too much fun, enjoyed the sex and the sunshine and the company too much to sabotage us.

"Eddie?" Wish sets his hand on my leg. "Did you hear a word I said?"

"I'm a complicated guy," I blurt out. "I know I told you that already. I don't know if I can be good for you. I don't know if I can be what you need in a boyfriend."

"Whoa, where did this come from? And maybe we should stop the car if you're going to break up with me." He leaves his hand on my thigh, and I reach down and take it in my own.

"I'm not—" I pull over anyway, into the weed-strewn gravel lot of a church, put the car in park, and turn to face him. "I'm not trying to break up with you. I don't know what I'm doing."

He considers me, all serious and seriously pretty, and he squeezes my hand, and oh my God, am I really starting a relationship with a twenty-four-year-old?

"Let's start small," he says. "Do you want to see me again?"

"Yes. I want that a lot."

"Okay. I do too. Why are you worried about being a complicated guy? I like *you*."

I take a deep breath. "My relationships don't tend to last because I'm high maintenance. I'm an incorrigible flirt. I don't tone down my big gay attitude for anyone, anywhere, so you can totally expect me to fag out and embarrass you in front of your straight friends."

"Fag out? Best you can do?" He laughs. "Okay, first of all, I like your big gay attitude. It's a turn-on to be with someone who doesn't give a fuck what anyone thinks. Second of all, the flirting is cute, especially when you do it with me. And I'm pretty sure 'high maintenance' is a code word for 'likes attention' and I like paying attention to you."

"I do like attention." I try to keep a straight face, but who am I kidding? "And I really like attention from you. And your cock."

He grins back at me. "So, we're good here? Your little crisis is over?"

"You know, there aren't a lot of people who are willing to put up with me on a regular basis."

"Well, that number grew by one, okay?" He undoes his seatbelt and leans across the console. He puts one hand on either side of my lap and kisses me.

It's not a "we're okay now" peck. It's a no-holds-barred sensual onslaught. It's teeth, tongue, perfect pressure. It's the kind of kiss that ends with clothes on the floor and somebody getting dicked out up against the wall.

It's the kind of kiss that makes promises.

"Fuck." I groan as he pulls out of the kiss and sits back in his seat. He fastens his seatbelt again and faces forward, brushing his hair out of his eyes and smiling like that cat who got the cream.

"You're pleased with yourself," I huff as I put the car in drive again.

"Just pleased." He starts fucking whistling, so off-key that it takes me a minute to recognize the song. "Blue Skies."

"You're a pretty great guy, Wish," I tell him as I pull into traffic. "But you got no fucking ear for music."

"Not one bit. Nobody wants to stand next to me when the singing starts at birthday parties."

"I think I'll keep you anyway."

chapter SIX

On Monday morning, I start making calls about the roads bill. No time like the present to thwart Romeo. I call my mother first because I know she'll start harping on it to her girlfriends in the active adult community where she lives. They're all about keeping Lake Lovelace a small, family-oriented town; especially since most of them grew up here when the town was first being built. It's *their* town, and as far as they're concerned, progress of any kind needs to wait until they're dead, so they can turn over in their graves.

Mama is properly scandalized.

After promising her I'm doing my best to preserve the nature of our community, I ask her about her best friend, Karen, who recently had a hip replacement. Karen's nephew works in the zoning commissioner's office.

"She says it's better than new—says she's going to dance the rumba at the Christmas party this year." Mama cackles into the phone. "I can't wait to see that. She'll be so touched you asked."

"Does her nephew still work for the city?"

"He does, and I'll be sure he gets an earful about this bridge project. Four lanes of traffic each direction? That's just wrong, honey."

"Too right, Mama."

"Did you know that Karen's youngest son, the one who lives in Miami, is gay?"

I wince. Yeah, I knew. I've known since the guy gave me a blowjob during the town Christmas tree lighting ceremony twenty years ago.

I have tried on many occasions to explain the "you don't out anyone, ever" rule to my mama, but she doesn't get it. "I may have known."

"Well, he finally came out to Karen and Geoff, so there's no reason for him to stay in Miami. I mean, now that everyone knows the truth."

Oh, I can see where this is headed. I take a deep breath and pray for patience.

"He has a job, a partner, a life in Miami. Don't start playing matchmaker in the hopes he'll move back home to cement the dynasty of two Lake Lovelace families, okay?"

Her put-upon sigh makes me smile. Mama is nothing if not relentless in her pursuit of my happiness—preferably the coupled variety.

"Edward Anthony Russell, I may be an old lady but I can still whip your ass for sassing me."

"Yes, Mother."

"Come to dinner Thursday, I'll make lasagna."

I glance at the calendar. "What time?"

"At dinnertime, Ed. And would it kill you to bring a date?"

She always asks, and I think it breaks her heart a little when I show up alone. I suppose I could bring Wish. He's made it clear he wants to have something like a relationship. Something more than smoking-hot sex. Well, meeting Mama would certainly show my willingness to try this dating thing at least.

"I've been seeing someone. I'll ask him. But Mama—" I pause for her squeals of joy. "Mama, it's not serious. We're casual."

"I serve him lasagna, he won't be casual for long. Oh, baby." She sounds like she's going to cry. "Bringing a man home to meet your mother. I'm so happy."

In spite of my attempt to deflate her expectations, by the time we hang up I think she's picking out a mother-of-the-groom dress.

Next, I start riling up the libertarians about the sin taxes. Romeo may be able to count on them to help him push cuts for social programs, but they aren't going to be happy about a tax increase. By the time six o'clock rolls around and I start my drive home from the marina, I feel like I've spent more time planting the seeds of an opposition to the road expansion than I have on my actual business endeavors. I use the Bluetooth to voice dial Wish.

"Hey, you." His voice is low and husky. Intimate. My breath catches and a rush of heat floods my groin.

"Hey, yourself. I promised my mother I would invite you to dinner on Thursday. You in?"

"You have a mother?"

"I didn't erupt, fully formed, from my daddy's head like Athena. Yes, I have a mother."

"And I get to meet her? That's a big deal, S-Class." There's as much excitement as nerves in his tone. God, he's as bad as she is. They're going to love each other.

"Are you afraid to meet my mother?" I'm oddly charmed by that.

"No."

"You should be." I laugh. "She's a feisty old lady, and she has no filter. She'll embarrass both of us, and her dog will pee on your shoes."

"She sounds terrific." He chuckles into the phone. "I'm in."

I pick him up at six thirty Thursday night. The GPS leads me to a newish apartment complex on the western side of town—about as far from the water as one can get and still be in Lake Lovelace proper. I park the Benz and make my way to the fourth floor—Jesus, you'd have to be young to live here. I'm in decent shape, but my knees would have a thing or two to say about a daily workout like that.

"Hey, S-Class." He greets me with a smile and a kiss on the cheek. I angle for a little more, but he pulls back and opens the door. "C'mon in; I'll be ready in a minute."

I step through the door into a small, but clean apartment. A young man in a baseball cap reclines on the sofa in the living room, playing a first-person shooter game, and a woman with long black hair is cooking at the stove.

"Eddie, this is my roommate, Jordan, and his girlfriend, Trinity. Guys, this is Eddie." He waves at the other people in his apartment, then disappears into another room.

"Pleasure to meet you." I nod at the girl, who gives me a bright smile, then the guy on the sofa, who sort of grunts at me.

Roommate. Ugh. So much for the possibility of postdinner coitus. The last time I had a roommate was when I let Ben live in my house nine years ago. Not an ideal situation, but it did help him get sober. I can't imagine voluntarily living with someone I wasn't fucking.

Stepping from one foot to the other, I listen to the buzz of an electric shaver until Wish emerges from the bathroom.

"Ready?" I ask, raising an eyebrow. God, he's pretty. I'd gotten used to his end-of-the-day scruff, but clean-shaven? He's even hotter.

"Absolutely. 'Night you guys." He waves at his roommate.

"What's that like?" I gesture back toward the apartment as I unlock the car. "Roommate?"

He shrugs. "Necessary evil. I don't really make enough to live on my own and save money too, so, Jordan."

Wow. I couldn't have asked for a clearer demonstration of how we're in different stages of life, compounded by the fact I've never had to worry about money. How the hell is this ever going to work?

"I don't know what that's like," I admit. "I'm a spectacularly privileged fucker."

He laughs. "I won't hold it against you."

But I can't help being unnerved by the reminder of our age difference as we head toward my mom's house. Wish doesn't seem to mind the silence though—he runs his hand up and down my thigh, almost absently like he's feeling the texture of my jeans. Finally, he says, "What's on your mind?"

"You're so . . ."

"Young."

I wince and nod.

"It's okay to notice it, you know? The difference. It doesn't bother me though. It's part of what I like about you. That you've lived a completely different life than I have, and we can still find common ground."

"That's the boner talking, lovely."

He laughs. "See, that's what I mean. You're funny and sexy, and I don't have to have been born in the sixties to see that, or to like it."

"It's going to piss you off at some point. There's going to be a final straw, where I'm too old, and it's just too weird for you."

"That's your baggage. Not mine. I'm not carrying it for you either, because that bag is toxic. Waiting for the other shoe to drop? Throw the damned thing and be done with it."

"You have quite the way with words," I say as we pull up to a stoplight, and he leans across the console and kisses me, deep and sweet. When a horn sounds behind us, we separate, and I blush as I drive through the intersection. "And kisses. You have a way with those too."

"That's the boner talking."

When Mama opens the door, her Jack Russell terrier, Ricochet, runs up my legs and then over to the couch, jumps on it, spins in a circle, leaps down, and runs over to Wish and circles him a few times before lifting his leg. I tug Wish out of the way, and he manages to avoid getting pee on his shoes. Mama clucks and fusses and scolds the dog, then puts him out back and returns to the door.

"Told you he'd pee on you," I whisper.

"Hi, honey." Mama greets me with a hug.

"Mama, this is Aloysius Carver. Wish, this is my mother, Maria Russell."

She stands back and gives him a dramatic up-down once-over, and he takes a step backward and does the same. Mama barks out a laugh and pulls him into a hug as well.

"Edward, I like this one," she says. "He's funny."

"Yeah he is." I grin at him. "I like him too."

He reaches out and squeezes my hand.

"I hope you like lasagna!" Mama calls over her shoulder as we follow her to the kitchen. She has a big formal dining room, but prefers the eat-in kitchen with its floor-to-ceiling-windowed breakfast nook. The smell of her Bolognese sauce permeates the air, making my stomach growl in anticipation. Lord ha'mercy, I love my mama's lasagna.

"Honey, open a bottle of that Sangiovese in the wine rack," she orders, opening the oven.

I do as I'm told, and pour three glasses, which I place on the already-set table. I catch Wish staring at me with a bemused expression on his face.

"What?" I ask.

"Nothing." He holds up his hands. "No comment."

"Bread, Edward." Mama points to the loaf sitting on a cutting board, and I start slicing it. This time, Wish doesn't stifle a laugh. Mama pauses in her fussing over the lasagna to give him a look.

"I've never seen him take orders from anyone without picking a fight," he explains.

"Well, in this house, Mama is boss. Watch out, she'll have you making a salad next."

"That's an excellent idea." She pulls out another cutting board and hands it to him. "The veggies are in the fridge."

He laughs and gets to work, and once everything is ready, we all move over to the table.

No sooner have we begun to eat than she launches into me about the roads project.

"Karen says Jeremy thinks the council is pretty divided on the project. Some think it's a good thing for the city, but others think the sin taxes are an unfair burden on the lowest-income residents."

Unfair burden. I hadn't thought about that angle. "That's an interesting thought. How can we use that? Anytime you increase sales taxes, the burden is highest on working-class people. I wonder how we can convince them it's in their own best interest to vote against Romeo's proposal?"

Wish stifles a noise. I glance over at him, and his face is all red with sharp frown lines on his forehead. What's his problem? I raise an eyebrow at him, but he shakes his head and takes another bite of lasagna.

"Well, honey, you should call the guys over at the radio station and see if they'll do a drive time interview with you. You know how persuasive you can be."

"That's a fantastic idea, Mama."

"Your daddy would be so proud of how you really care about the town's character. That was always so important to him."

"Thanks, Mama."

I swallow around the lump in my throat. My father and I had a complicated relationship right up until his death a few years ago. His approval was hard won, and his work ethic was second to none. If Mama says he'd be proud, he probably would be. I flush a little, and I try not to let the praise go to my head, but I can't help it—some little boys might outgrow wanting their daddy's approval, but I never did.

As though she can sense that I need a moment, Mama turns to Wish. "And what do you do for a living, Aloysius?"

"Please, call me Wish." He smiles at her, then turns a glare on me. "I work in road construction."

Oh, shit.

How on Earth did I forget that bit of information?

Embarrassment colors my face, and I take a deep drink of water. I cannot believe how badly I've fucked this up. I didn't even consider Wish's work—or his working-class income—when the conversation began. No wonder he was so uncomfortable. I'm such an asshole.

The three of us stare at the table, the silence growing awkward. Finally, Mama speaks. "How long have you been doing that?"

"I've worked road crews since I graduated high school, so six years now. I also work part-time at my brother's body shop when he needs a hand, but road work is my main gig."

"Well, that's very . . ." She turns to me for help, but I'm still speechless with my own horror. "That's nice."

Wish glances at me, clears his throat, and looks back at my mother.

"It was really nice to meet you, Mrs. Russell. Eddie, I'm not feeling so great; do you think you could take me home?"

chapter SEVEN

he doesn't speak again as I say good-bye to my mother. He simply walks out of her house, and I find him a few moments later, standing by the passenger door of my car. I tap the door release button on my keys, and he pulls the door open and sits down, slamming it behind him. I wince. Yes, just a few weeks ago, I wasn't interested in a relationship. But now? Now that I have one and it's been threatened by my own stupidity, it seems desperately important to protect it. And yeah, he might be acting a little petulant, but I really can't blame him.

"Wish, I'm sor—" I start to apologize as I slide into the seat.

"Don't." He makes a short gesture with his hand. "I realized you were rich and privileged and that you lived a completely different life than I do. I didn't realize you were a snob."

"I'm not . . ."

He silences me with a glare.

"Okay, that's probably fair," I continue. "But I didn't think about what you do for a living when the topic of conversation came up. I didn't think—"

"My boss has the countywide contract for roadwork. That project is job security for me. That project means I can stay in Lake Lovelace with my family. And you're opposed to it because you don't want to pay an extra two percent tax on your fifty-dollar bottles of wine?"

"It's not about money. It's about—"

"The 'character of the town.'" He makes air quotes as he says it. "Bullshit."

Okay, so maybe it is a little bit. The rhetoric of politics. But that doesn't mean the expansion is good for the town, or that I won't be affected.

"My boat dealership is located at the site of the proposed bridge expansion," I admit. "So I do have a personal stake. But it's also true that the tax increase will be hardest on working-class consumers. Like the people who go to Keith's club. Like you."

"Oh no, this isn't for my own good, don't even. Keeping both of my jobs so I can afford to live in a crappy apartment near my family is more important than avoiding a tiny tax increase. As for your dealership: you can't afford to move it?"

That so isn't the point, and he knows it.

"I shouldn't have to move it! There's been a dealership on that site since we built this lake."

"We? *You* weren't even alive then, let alone me."

"I meant the founders. My grandfather was one of them." I flush. Using the royal we after being called a snob wasn't going to get me out of the hot seat.

"But you *could* move it. Do you know how hard it is to find a road job near my family? My mom is only six months cancer-free, and I don't want to move halfway across the state. Her medical bills are insane, and the only way Max can afford to help her with them is because I don't let him pay me a fair wage for the work I do in his shop. You've obviously never had to worry about money in your life, but Jesus, Eddie, how about a little empathy?"

"It's not only me, you know. I have employees. People like Ben. They count on that dealership for work too."

"Oh, how could I forget Ben?" he snaps. "Of course, Ben needs you. Ben counts on you. Ben walks into your bedroom on a Saturday morning as if he belongs there."

I flinch, but it's not like I can deny ever having slept with Ben. "Jealousy is not a good look for you, lovely. And Ben is only one of my employees. Jerry has three kids in college for God's sake."

"And I don't doubt for a moment that you could find a way to take care of them."

"Hell, lovely, if it's about job security, I can give *you* a job."

He opens and closes his mouth a few times, then shakes his head. "You were concerned about awkward power dynamics because of our age difference. You don't think it would be worse if you were my *boss*?"

"If the choice is between leaving town and working for me, I'd hope you would consider me the lesser of two fucking evils, all right?"

"Just take me home." He twists away.

He's absolutely silent for the rest of the drive. I try to draw him into conversation, to apologize again, but each foray is met with another death-glare, and finally I give up. When I pull up in front of his building, he's already got the seatbelt unbuckled.

"Wish. Please." I put my hand on his arm.

"What?" he snarls.

"I truly am sorry. I know we don't see eye to eye on this, but please, don't . . ." *don't leave me like this.*

He pauses a long moment, glaring at me, then shakes his head. "Give my apologies to your mother. Good night, Eddie."

How does one woo back the boyfriend he wasn't sure he wanted in the first place?

And why is it so goddamned important all of a sudden? I didn't even want a relationship with him. I only wanted hot, kinky sex. But he makes me laugh, and he's the best kind of eye candy, and he gets me, really fucking gets me the way few people ever have. It's not just that he gets my kinks. He gets the risk-taking. The wakeboarding, the picking fights. He sasses me back. He came to see me in the hospital because I was bored. Those things that seemed like reasons not to push him away have become reasons to hold him close.

I don't think a dick pic is gonna cut it.

I start with a text the next morning, because I'm not very good at judging exactly how badly I blew it. When you aren't used to boyfriends, you're not used to fucking shit up either.

I'm sorry. Can we talk about it?

There. Straight, to the point, sincere. Mostly. I'm not entirely sure which part of the whole fiasco I'm sorry for. Sorry he left, sorry we don't agree, sorry we didn't have sex last night . . . *shit.* None of it is really an apology.

How did I get to be forty-four years old without learning how to apologize properly?

It all turns out to be moot because he doesn't reply. I'm pissed now, because here I am, agonizing over how to make it up to him, and he doesn't even text back. After checking my messages for the eight millionth time in an hour, I toss my phone down on the desk and head out for a walk.

The second I step outside in the sweltering heat, I start to regret my choice. Russell Marina is, by necessity, right on the water, and the humidity here is enough to choke a man. Even in a polo shirt and khakis, I start sweating immediately.

"Caleb," I call to the kid running the boats from storage to the docks, "put my MasterCraft in."

He nods and runs off to fetch my boat. A few minutes later, he's got it in the water, and I'm off. Much better than a walk for clearing the head. I cruise along aimlessly until I find myself pulling up behind the dealership. Dave's Range Rover is parked out front, which means he's probably there with Ben. A funny twinge in my chest makes me turn the boat around. As much as I would appreciate their advice, the sappy togetherness is too much for me to handle today. And it's not even like they're ridiculous about it, but sometimes I see the way Ben watches Davis and I wonder what it would take to get a man to look at me like I'm the last bottle of water in the desert.

I head back to the marina and my silent phone.

The next morning, I try again, early this time, hoping to get him before he goes to work.

I didn't mean to hurt you, and I regret that. I'd like to see you. Call me back?

But he doesn't.

So I take a shower, and I try not to be disappointed, in myself, in him, in how craving him in my life crept up on me and how not having him hurts.

And of course the phone is ringing when I step out. I stub my toe in the rush to the bedroom to answer it, and I bite back a curse.

"Hello?"

"It's. Um, it's me . . . Wish."

Hope is a big, bright thing unfurling in my chest. "Hi. I'm so glad you called."

"I need you to let me be mad for a while, okay? Maybe stop with the texts. I mean, I appreciate the apology, but I'm still pissed at you."

"I know. And I want to make it right."

He sighs. "I don't know how to say this except—I don't know if *you* can fix it. But I know *I* can't be with you when I feel this way. It's different from the riling each other up for play. Because we play rough, it's important to be clear where the lines are and not risk bringing genuine anger into our play. If I ever hurt you for real, I'd hate myself. You get that, right?"

God. Even when he's mad at me, he's so fucking sweet.

"I don't want it to be over," I whisper.

"I don't either," he admits. "So give me a few days. Don't text, don't call; let me stew in my own juices, okay?"

That's going to be hard. Really fucking hard. But I can do it.

"Okay," I agree.

It takes three days. Three goddamn fucking days of thinking about him and being sad and angry and remorseful all at once. Three days of wanting him and not having him. Three days of holding back.

When my phone finally rings, my nerves almost knock me off my chair. I'm at the pro shop, having lunch with Ben, and I take the phone to the back office, walking on shaky legs.

"I wasn't sure you were going to call."

"I think we need to talk about it, clear the air."

"I can do that."

"And then, I think we need to figure out how to disagree like grown-ups and move on."

"I can do that too." Relief washes over me.

"I'll come over tonight then? To talk?"

"Absolutely. Should I get dinner delivered?"

"Let's see how the talk goes."

Ah. There it is. The acknowledgment that talking might not be enough. Disappointment leaves a bitter taste in my mouth. "Okay."

"Seven sound good?"

I nod, realize he can't see me, then manage, "Yes."

"I'll see you then."

When I walk back out into the shop, Ben is with a customer. I take my seat behind the counter and pick up my sandwich. Unfortunately, my appetite seems to be mostly gone, so I watch Ben charm the customer with a story about some sick air he got one time. Ben's anecdotes almost always turn into a sale. Sure enough, a few minutes later the girl comes to the counter with a new board and bindings and a starry-eyed expression on her face. Ben grins while I ring up her order, that sweet, contagious grin of a guy talking about something he loves. I don't know if he knows how appealing he is when he talks about his sport, how anyone who sees him when he describes cutting through the water falls for him, but I'd say the girl is firmly in the Legend fan club by the time she leaves.

"Nice kid." Ben gestures at her with his chin, settling in next to me and resuming his lunch.

"You had her completely charmed."

"She was getting frustrated with her board. Wants bigger air. The three-stage rocker in the new board will be good for her."

I feel a pang at the thought of the shop not being here. At the idea of it moving somewhere else, or simply being . . . gone. What Ben's made of the place is special. He's good for this town and for the kids who idolize him. He shows them what a living legend can be—a part of a community, a cornerstone of it even.

And never mind the community; what would happen to Ben without the dealership? He doesn't have a college degree, and he can't exactly make a living wakeboarding anymore. He can't meet the lifting requirements for a lot of retail jobs and manual labor is completely out of the question. How the hell would someone like Ben survive unemployment?

"Wish and I had a fight."

He sets his sandwich down. "You break up?"

"I don't know; were we even together?" I wave a hand at him. "And I don't know. He's coming over tonight to talk."

"Good. You'll sort it out. He seems like a good guy."

"He is." I fidget in my chair. "Hey, Ben?"

He grunts and raises an eyebrow at me.

"Did you know anything about me before we met?"

"Nope. Heard people calling you a fag. Figured you were a guy I'd like to know." He leers at me.

I can't help but laugh. Man, I got a lot of ass in high school. The benefits of being the only gay guy out. "Yeah. I'm glad."

"Me too. I got blowjobs from your exes."

I feel a little wistful. It had been a rough, angry time in my life, but it had also been exhilarating. My first taste of power. My first understanding of how I could fit into this town as more than my daddy's son.

"Would you be mad if I told him a secret I haven't even told you?"

Ben startles. "You have secrets?"

I look away for a minute. "Yeah. A few."

"I think it's a good thing, you wanting to tell him something personal. I think that's real good."

"It won't hurt your feelings?"

He slings an arm over my shoulder, gives me a snuggle. "Eddie, I want you to have what Dave and I have. I want you to find someone who makes you feel alive and full of hope and joy. And who puts stripes on your ass—because I know you like that sort of thing." He shudders and holds up a hand. "Not judging. I just . . ."

"Yeah."

"I know I gave you a rough time about him at first, but I like the idea of you having someone."

"Thanks." I lean into his shoulder, enjoying the closeness.

"Welcome."

He gives me one last squeeze, and then lets go before the hug gets awkward. "So, this kid, what's he got that he managed to tame the notorious Edward Russell?"

"He makes me happy." I shrug.

"That's all that really matters, isn't it?"

The doorbell rings right at seven. I love his punctuality. I open it to find him standing on the front porch, a bottle of wine in hand. "It's cheap." He holds it up. "But I thought if we ended up ordering in, it would be nice to have a glass of wine with dinner."

"Thanks." I take the bottle. His bringing wine is a good sign, right? Hopeful, at the very least.

"Let's go sit down." I take his hand and lead him to the living room, and I sit in the corner of the gigantic sectional and curl my feet under me, setting the bottle down on the way.

"Come here." I pat the couch next to me. "I want to tell you something. It might seem a little out of context, but I promise, I have a point."

He sits, all tension and rough angles.

"When I was sixteen, I was working at what was then the Russell-Romeo Marina. My dad and Rodney Romeo's uncle were business partners. My summer job, such as it was, was running odd jobs around the place."

Wish starts to settle into the story, and I pull his feet into my lap. He's initially resistant, but he gives in as I keep talking.

"I had a secret. A boyfriend. He was older—twenty-one—and an intern in the accounting department. He was so funny, and sweet, and really the perfect first boyfriend to explore my sexuality with." I slip off his shoes and begin to massage his feet.

"Ben wasn't your first?"

"No, I met him later. Thank God." I smile. "Justin was my first, and he was something else. I was starting to figure out I liked it rough. I didn't know what masochism was, beyond some porn that turned me on for reasons I didn't understand. Justin wasn't a sadist or a Dom even—I honestly don't think he was kinky at all. But when I told him to pull my hair and slap me around a little while I was blowing him, he was game. He was really game for anything that made me happy."

"He sounds great."

"He was." I squeeze his feet in my lap. He's much more relaxed now and doesn't protest. "Anyway, Rodney Romeo was at the marina to pick up his boat, and he came into the office. I remember everything about that day. It was hot and sticky, and I had Justin's pants around his ankles under the desk while I blew him. The room smelled like my dad's cigarettes and sunscreen. Romeo's keys hit the floor behind me right at the exact moment that Justin yanked my hair and came in my mouth. It was the first time he'd done that—come without warning me—and he pulled my hair hard enough that I shot too. Knowing someone had walked in on us made it hotter—for about the time it took for my dick to stop spurting all over the floor."

"Then what happened?"

The humiliation and pain of that afternoon sweep over me, and I can't meet his eyes. I sniff hard, trying to hold back the prickling sensation in my face.

"He outed us both. To my dad. To his uncle. Justin got fired, and my dad threatened to have him arrested for statutory rape. My whole life changed that afternoon. And while I don't regret who I am or what I've done with myself . . . I felt like I'd lost a lot more than my boyfriend. And he lost a lot more than an internship."

"How did your dad take it?"

I always feel a pang when I think about my dad. "He called me into his office after he fired Justin, and he stared at me for a while. Then he said we were rich enough I could fuck who I wanted and no one would care, but I should probably stick to guys my own age, and to wrap it up for God's sake, hadn't I ever heard of AIDS?" I smile at the memory, even though I'd been terrified at the time. I had it about as good as any queer kid in the eighties ever did. "I wish I could have told him myself."

"I'm sorry, Eddie."

"Not your fault." I let him see it then, the way I suit up. I straighten my spine and deliberately jut my chin. "You see, lovely, that's something that can only be taken from a person once. In a way, Romeo did me a favor. Yes, he outed me to my dad, but I never had to come out ever again. I claimed my queerness with every breath I took. By the time I went back to school at the end of the summer, there was a new swish to my step, a lilt to my voice, and a violence under my skin. I heard every slur in the world the first week, but nobody laid a finger on me. I practically dared them. I was itching for a fight, but no one gave it to me."

"That's probably a good thing. But I'm still sorry you went through that."

"I'm not." I mean it. "It was awful, but it made me king of this town. Whether they left me alone because they respected me or because they were afraid of me, I'm not sure. But they did, and I thrived."

I give his feet a final squeeze. "Unfortunately, Rodney Romeo and I have been at war ever since. His uncle and my dad parted ways. His mama and my mama stopped playing tennis together. The roads project? It's no accident they chose *that* bridge to propose expansion, when there's another one three miles away which is on a bigger highway and has more traffic. It's personal for me. I let it become an obsession. I'm sorry I didn't consider your feelings."

He sighs. "I still support the project. I have to. But I get how personal this is for you. I'm sorry I called you a snob."

"Oh, I think I deserved that." I shift so that I can set his feet down and then I crawl onto his lap. I straddle him on my knees and stare into his eyes. Neither one of us is hard, and that's okay. Since I don't see any more anger in his face, I relax, laying my head on his shoulder. "I want us to give this a try. Lovers—boyfriends—whatever you want to call it, I want to do it with you. I want to introduce you to my mom, for real. I want to meet your mom and your brother. And didn't you say you have a cat? I want to meet her too."

His hands come up and stroke along my spine. "I'd like that."

"So we can agree to disagree? About the roads?"

He nods. "For now. In November, when we vote on the tax, it'll change things."

"I know."

"Okay."

He keeps stroking me, and I shiver. I lift my head and claim his lips, trying to show him how relieved and thankful I am for the reunion. I slide my hand around the side of his neck, feeling his pulse hammering and his muscles flexing. He runs his hands down my back to cup my ass, rocking me forward into his dick, which, like mine, is stiffening fast. I break the kiss, and he chases after it, biting my lower lip.

"God, I missed this," he murmurs, then he tugs me back in for another.

His kisses are the kind that go on and on, a heady, mind-reeling seduction with lips and tongue and even teeth. The whole time, he never stops rocking our hips together, first slowly, but then more urgently as we start to get really into it.

I pull away again, this time putting a hand between us when he'd drag me back.

"Skin," I demand, and he rips off his shirt, then mine, and then lifts me off his lap and dumps me on the couch, reaching for the button on my pants. I try to help him, but he slaps my hands away, hauling my pants off and then stripping himself of his own. He leans over me, a wicked grin on his face. "You're so fucking hot. How do you want to do this? If you're feeling vanilla, we could move to the bedroom, but I'd love to warm your ass up with my hand and play with your balls before I fuck you over this couch."

I groan. I do want it—especially whatever he's got intended for my balls—but the idea of folding myself across his lap angers me as much as it turns me on. I shake my head. "Not vanilla."

He sits and hauls me across his lap, facedown. He slaps my ass hard three times, then runs his hand over it, moaning softly. "God, your ass. My handprint. This is the sexiest thing I've ever seen."

Stunned, I let him spank me again, several more times, while I grind my dick into the space between his thighs. Heat washes over me, and it takes me a minute to figure out it's not the spanking that's turning me on as much as how he gets off on marking me with his hand. I groan and buck into it.

"Harder," I whisper, and he gives it to me.

Every few slaps, he rubs my ass and I rut into his lap, making wild, needy noises. Then, after one flurry of spanks, he reaches between my legs and grabs my balls—not gently, either. I go very, very still as my anticipation spikes.

"Are you okay?" he asks, ever so slightly tightening his grip. "You can safeword anytime."

I nod, taking a deep breath, all my attention zeroing in on the feeling of his big hand wrapped around my tender flesh.

His hand tightens.

It hurts, not the playful sting of the spanking, but a deep, scary hurt. He has my goddamn testicles in his fist and he's squeezing.

It's terrifying. He could really damage me. But it's fucking hot as hell too. For me, cock and ball torture requires a profound trust, an intimacy beyond what we've done before. I'm completely helpless and vulnerable for him, and nothing is sexier than that.

Adrenaline races through me, hopefully bringing endorphins on its heels. I breathe through the pain as his fist tightens again, and I shudder. My whole body is prickly and extra sensitive.

"One more, honey," he whispers, and I can't help it, as the pressure intensifies, I squirm and gasp, and a sob is wrenched out of me. He loosens his grip slowly, then rubs my ass, sweet words spilling from his lips, punctuated with "holy fucks" and "so hots" until he turns me over and lays me back on the couch.

The rough upholstery fabric abrades my ass, but his body on mine, the press of skin and muscle, feels so good, I start to cry. I can't remember the last time I let a lover push me so hard without safewording.

He shushes into my hair, running his hands over me. "So good, honey. So hot. Thank you. I love that you trust me so much." He grabs my cock and starts pumping it. My abused balls ache even as they draw up in anticipation of orgasm.

"Fuck me, please," I beg, thrusting my cock into his fist, chasing more sensation any way I can get it.

"Condoms?"

"Gah." I slap the back of the couch, frustrated. "Upstairs."

"I'm not letting go of your dick until you come," he says, "but lift your legs."

I pull my knees back and hold them tight to my chest as he drops to his knees on the floor. He makes a liar of himself, letting go of my dick long enough to rotate my body so my ass is right in his face before grabbing it again. This time, as he jerks me, I feel a tug on my guiche ring. I watch him, wishing I could actually see it in his teeth. My balls draw up impossibly tight. He lets go and then licks gently at my hole.

"Gonna fuck this hole with my tongue. I want to hear you scream. Don't you dare hold back those noises, Eddie. You get me so fucking hot."

And then he shoves a dry finger into me, making me arch off the couch in surprise. He goes to town on my ass, licking and fingering me while jerking me with his other hand.

I groan, helpless and heated, letting him have everything, anything he wants. If he wants me to make noise, I'll give him every moan and gasp.

When he finds my prostate with that teasing finger, my voice goes sharp and fluttery. He starts pressing on it, then sliding his finger over it, then pressing again. Holy *fuck*, that feels *good*.

My climb to orgasm is a terrifying, thrilling leap into sensation. My balls throb in pain as I come, catapulting my pleasure into a whole new realm of bliss. Convulsing, drawn tight by both pleasure and pain, I tuck my face into my shoulder and let myself go.

Over the next few moments, I return to myself with his hands still on my body. I sit up, reaching for him, and he glides from the floor into my arms like it's his favorite place to be. Grabbing his cock, I pump it in my hand, and he pushes me back until I'm lying on the couch again, his body pressed close, my hand moving between us the only sound in the room.

"Fuck." His head drops down, and he watches me jerk him. He moves his hand over mine, showing me without words the rhythm he likes. My breath catches as he throws his head back and lets out a desperate growl.

He comes without a warning, a splash of his cum hitting my face; another paints the arm of the couch. He twists and arches, fucking my hand for all he's worth until he collapses on top of me.

"Holy shit." He groans, struggling to control his breathing. When he manages, he kisses me until he's lost it again. I laugh into his mouth, high as a kite and fuzzy-headed from the pain and release. Subspace—what a blissful thing. When I start shaking, he yanks my velour throw off the back of the couch and wraps us both in it as he massages my ass and snuggles me tighter.

"You're so fucking good, honey."

We don't get to the wine or ordering takeout until much, much later.

chapter EIGHT

We fall into a routine as easy as breathing.

Weekdays are hit or miss, depending on our schedules, but weekends are a glorious mess of sex and laughter, ending Monday mornings with me pulling a pillow over my eyes while he does yoga. Most Mondays. The last Monday in August is different.

"What are you doing Labor Day weekend?" I ask as I pour our coffee, not making eye contact. It's five in the morning; I glare at the ruddy sky out the window. It's too freaking early to be up, but I wanted to catch him before he left for work, so when he finished his sun salutations, I hopped out of bed and followed him downstairs, babbling about how *some* couples have coffee together.

"Don't know. Was gonna see what Max is up to." The brother. Family time. I'm dying of curiosity about them. We made up, and that was great, but the whole "meet each other's families" thing has come to a screeching halt. Probably because conversation topics that mention either of our jobs have been strictly off-limits—in the name of keeping peace.

"Would you like to go to the wakeboarding tournament with me? It's a big local thing. I'm going to watch from the cabin cruiser out on the lake. Max and his wife and your mom are welcome to join us. I'd love to meet them."

"That sounds fun. I guess Ben and Dave will be there too?"

I turn around to face him. "No, not this time. Ben is emceeing the event, and Dave is going to be out of town. He's designing some house in the desert. I can ask Tina to come though, if you'd like someone to explain the finer points of technique."

His face brightens a little. "And your mom?"

"The idea of Ricochet and Elvis together on my boat scares the bejesus out of me, but sure." A series of mental images ends with a for sale sign hung from the hull of my devastated cruiser, but if it makes him happy . . .? *Damn*, I must really want to make him happy.

He laughs, then comes around the counter and wraps me in his arms. "I'll ask them today. Thank you for inviting us."

I snuggle into his embrace for a minute, then reach for the coffee. "Just let me know how many say yes so I can give the caterer a head count."

His arms stiffen around me. What did I say? *Caterer.* I need a list of "privileged-motherfucker words to avoid." I set the coffee back down without drinking it, and rush to reassure him.

"It's not like that. It's basically call-ahead takeout. Bagged lunches. The boat kitchen is way too small to cook for more than two people."

He relaxes again. "I'll get used to it, I guess. Being pampered by my rich boyfriend. Max is gonna tease the crap out of me."

"That's what brothers do. It builds character or something."

"Let me guess, you're an only child?"

"You knew that already."

"*Max* is the reason I joined the wrestling team in high school. Once I learned how to throw his ass to the ground, he miraculously outgrew the pushy-older-brother shtick."

"And I get to reap the benefits. *Mercy.*" I drop a wink on him, and he laughs, palming my ass with one hand.

"I'll throw this ass to the ground anytime you like."

"Please." I purr, kissing the side of his throat. He groans, and his grip on my waist tightens, then he lets me go and puts a little space between us. Breathing room because, no lie, that wrestling talk gets us both hard.

"After work." He casts a glance at the clock on the microwave. "I'll call you later?"

"Sure."

He gives me a thoroughly lush and decadent good-bye kiss, followed by a bruising pinch to my nipple. I suspect I'll spend most of the day with an erection from remembering it.

When he calls me early that evening, his voice is ragged and beyond exhausted. "They said yes."

"Fantastic. Are you okay? You sound like shit."

He huffs a laugh. "There was an accident at work today; I'm at the hospital."

Fear drives a sudden spike through me. "What kind of accident, were you hurt? What do you need?"

"*I'm* fine. One of my buddies, not so much. He's in the ICU in critical condition."

It's the absolute wreckage in his voice that gets me. "I'll come pick you up."

"Thank you." The words are low and fierce. "And, Eddie, can you bring me a shirt?"

I drive like a bat out of hell and practically throw my keys at the hospital valet. I stride through the hospital doors with a spare T-shirt in my hand, and I feel like I'm walking in slow motion, like a movie. It's not until I get to the front desk that I realize I've gone in the wrong part of the building. Emergency is on the other side.

"Is there a shortcut through here to emergency?" I ask the hospital concierge.

"Sure thing." She gives me directions through the hospital. "If the patient is in surgery, the friends and family will be waiting apart from general emergency waiting." She describes where I'm most likely to find the construction crew, and I take off at a run.

A few minutes later, my heart beats extra loudly in my chest as I round the corner into the waiting area and search the faces there for my hard-hat angel.

He's standing away from the other guys, a satellite to their group. When he looks up and notices me, I see that moment of indecision. He said once he wasn't in the closet, but I'd bet three of my savings accounts he's never engaged in a full-on PDA in front of his coworkers. So, instead of hugging him, I step up and put a hand on his shoulder, the way a brother or a friend would.

"You okay?" I speak close to his ear, and he nods once, a tight lift of his chin, and then the words burst free.

"Nobody really knows anything, but most of the guys are too worked up to care; they keep asking if they can donate blood and how soon will someone talk to us—his family is in a different waiting room, so my guess is never. The worksite has been closed down while they investigate the cause of the accident, so who knows how long it will be before we're back at work." He shudders and falls silent. Then, pointing at the shirt in my hand, asks, "Is that for me?"

I hand it over.

It's obvious he was close to whatever happened. His shirt is covered in blood and though his hands are red from scrubbing, he's still got stains under his fingernails.

"Pressure on the wound," he mutters, tugging his shirt off and dropping it at his feet. I get a glimpse of his lean torso, blessedly unscathed, before he yanks my shirt over his head. He picks up his shirt and stalks off to the nurses' station. One of them pulls on a glove and takes it, a moue of annoyance on her face.

"Are you Russell?" a squat man with a sun-lined face approaches me. He's probably younger than me, but harder living makes him appear older. He has an air of authority about him, like maybe he's a foreman or a supervisor. This day must be hell for the man in charge.

"Yeah, I'm sorry. Edward Russell." I reach out my hand to shake.

"Conlon." He pumps my hand once, not offering his first name. "You think you can find anything out for us about Tommy? I mean, your name is on part of this hospital, right?"

I groan inwardly. The cardiology wing, specifically, but that doesn't mean I can get around HIPAA. "I'm sorry, Mr. Conlon. I only gave them money; I don't actually have any way to find out . . ."

He nods. "I figured, but we owe it to Tommy to ask, right?" The other guys nod back.

Wish returns to my side. "Can you take me home?"

"Anything you want." I stop myself before adding an endearment.

"Hey, Conlon, call me if you hear anything, okay?"

"Yeah. Hey, thanks, man. For doing what you did out there."

Wish grunts, and I can tell he's itching to get away from this waiting room, so I put a steadying hand on his back and steer him toward the door. A chorus of weary "Later, Carvers" follows us.

As soon as we're out of sight of his coworkers, he leans against the wall and pulls me into a crushing hug.

"That was fucking awful," he says. "Goddamn Tommy."

"Are you okay?" I ask. "What do you need?"

"Oblivion." He lets go of me and then grabs my hand as we start walking toward the doors.

I thrust a credit card at the parking people and a moment later my car appears. I tip the valet the twenty that was in my wallet, and hope Wish doesn't see. I don't have any smaller bills, and I don't want to waste any time dealing with money.

I settle him into the passenger seat and take him home.

He protests when we get to my house instead of his apartment. Something about clothes.

"You can wear mine. We're about the same size." My T-shirts might be snug on him, but I'm sure my jeans will fit him fine.

"You wear jeans that cost half my paycheck."

"And you'll look damn fine in them, come on. Come inside, I'll feed you and put you to bed."

He follows me in, shoulders slumped and expression vacant. I send him upstairs to shower and open my fridge.

Takeout box. Takeout box. More takeout boxes. Don't I have any actual food? I glance at the calendar. Grocery delivery is on Tuesdays, so no, I really don't. There's a can of those exploding biscuits in the door of the fridge. I can't remember ever ordering them. I take those out and start heating the oven. A peek in the freezer rewards me with vacuum-sealed packs of steak. A corporate gift from god-knows-who, god-knows-when. I pull out a pair and toss them in the sink with warm water.

Vegetables. What the hell am I going to do about vegetables? I don't even have bagged salad in the fridge. Ever since I heard about people getting salmonella from that stuff, it's been out of the question. I open the pantry, dubious. I can't remember the last time I ate something from a can. All the normal kitchen stuff I never use is there: flour, sugar, baking powder. What's baking powder even for? A couple jars of salsa. I stare at those for a moment . . . salsa is kind of a vegetable, but we don't have any chips. It's not like we can eat it with a spoon.

"I don't have any vegetables," I announce to the pantry, which mocks me silently.

I turn around and see Wish standing there, barefoot in a pair of my sweats.

"Not that hungry."

"But you'll feel better if you eat." I settle him in at the kitchen table.

I manage to serve us up a pair of steaks and a plate of biscuits, and in spite of his protest, he eats everything I put in front of him before pushing away his plate and reaching for me.

I slip into his arms, clutching his head against my stomach and ruffling my fingers through his hair. The tension in his body and the anguished hitch in his breath gut me, and I tuck him closer to my body and rock him.

"They were moving sections of Jersey barrier, and somehow one wasn't clamped properly and it fell on him. A piece of rebar cut his thigh. It took the fire department half an hour to get there because of traffic on that narrow highway. I had to hold pressure on the wound while he screamed because no one else had the stomach for it."

"I'm sorry." Inadequate, but it feels worse to say nothing.

His arms tighten around me. "Even once the paramedics got there, they couldn't pull the barrier off him until the firefighters arrived, and he *still* might lose the leg."

"That's terrible." I stroke his hair again. "But he's lucky you were there." *Thank God it wasn't you.* It honestly didn't occur to me that his job was dangerous. I knew it was physical, but I didn't associate it with actual danger.

"It could have been me. It could have been any of us who work that part of the crew." He shudders, and I rub the back of his neck in small circles. It seems to calm him, being touched, so I keep up the massage.

"You want to go to bed?" I ask.

He slumps against me. "Yeah."

The dishes can wait until tomorrow. He lets me lead him upstairs, clinging to my hand like a lifeline. That trust touches me deeply, a sweet ache in my chest tinged with gratitude that I can do something for him that no one else can. I tuck him into my bed and spoon him from behind, taking the protective posture he normally would. He pulls my arm around him like armor, gripping my hand tightly against his belly. I kiss the back of his neck, willing the last bit of tension to slip from his body, and I hold him until we both fall asleep.

I wake up to him running his hand through *my* hair and studying me with a serious expression on his face. He's perched on the side of my bed, wearing my T-shirt and my oldest, most faded pair of jeans.

"Hi," I whisper.

"Good morning."

"Is it morning?" I yawn. "Too soon."

"The site is closed today." He holds up his phone. "Tommy's out of surgery for now, but probably needs another. They think they saved his leg."

I rub my eyes. "That's good."

"Yeah. Thanks for coming to pick me up yesterday. I wasn't holding it together too well."

"Of course. That's what boyfriends do. Are you okay?"

"I was really scared. Scared for Tommy. Scared for me. And that's *not* how I planned to introduce you to my coworkers." There's a flicker of a smile around his lips.

"You told them about me?" I remember Conlon knowing my name in the hospital.

"Yeah. I mean, they think your campaign against the roads project is shit—" we both wince "—but I told them you were an okay guy in spite of your politics. That led to me admitting I was dating you."

I laugh. "Hmm. An 'okay guy' doesn't exactly sound like a ringing endorsement."

"It's a macho environment. I don't keep the fact that I'm gay a secret, but I don't go bragging on my guy the way those guys talk about their girlfriends."

Ah. A choice I understand, even if it's not one I would make myself.

"You know, I'd love to get to know your friends. Why don't you invite some of them for Labor Day? I mean, you've met Ben and everyone, but I've only met your roommate. And only the one time."

He recoils a tiny bit. "I don't know that it's a good idea with everything that happened yesterday. Maybe another time."

I'm not sure what meeting me has to do with the events at his worksite, but I stifle my annoyance. He had a hellacious day; some incongruity can be forgiven.

"Okay, another time. What do you want to do today?" I tug him down to the bed as I change the subject. "I can take the day off. I have a conference call at two, but I can call in from anywhere."

"I'd like that." He smiles shyly, so unlike the confident Wish I know. I've seen him happy and horny and angry, but never vulnerable like yesterday or this morning. His armor is down, and he's letting me see. Something's changed.

"I like you like this too, you know," I whisper, and he flinches a little, then softens again.

"I don't want you to think I'm not . . ." he searches for the word, then settles on, "capable."

"Of course I don't think that. It takes a strong guy to admit he's scared."

He doesn't answer me, not with words anyway. Instead, he cups my face in his hands and he gives me a long and lazy kiss full of the best promise.

chapter NINE

the Saturday before Labor Day, I wake to an aching ass and Wish wrapped around me like we're velcroed together. Rolling out of his arms, I pad into the bathroom to take a long, hot shower and rinse away any leftover traces from last night's sexcapades, then I take stock of myself in the mirror. Meeting his family for the first time and I've got bruises on my ass. I glance at them and shudder at the memory of him digging his fingers into the marks he'd made with the skinny paddle I love. And yeah, that's a bite mark on my shoulder, complete with a scab where his tooth actually broke the skin. He was mortified, but it turned me on so much, his mortification didn't last long. When I told him he was in no danger of hearing my safeword from a love bite, he treated me to several more until I was a writhing, begging mess. God, he was so fucking hot. I'm starting to get hard just thinking about his teeth on my skin.

He's going to introduce me to his mother like this? I cross to the walk-in closet and open a drawer, digging for my board shorts. I own exactly one pair, and I save them for meeting people's families. Easing them on, I wince when they scrape over the tender skin of my ass. A short-sleeved cashmere T-shirt matches the purple in my board shorts—perfect. When I turn around, Wish is standing in the doorway to the bathroom, gloriously naked, scratching his chest and staring at me with a funny expression on his face.

"What are you wearing?" His voice is sleepy and confused.

"Shorts, love. I hear they're all the rage."

"What happened to those microscopic green Speedos you're so hot in?"

"They clash with the bruises." I raise an eyebrow. He can't seriously want me to wear those today. In front of his *mother*. With paddle marks on my ass.

"Eddie. I don't want you to pretend to be someone you're not for my family." He folds his arms over his chest.

Ah. *That's what this is about.*

"That's not what's happening." I lean on the doorframe to the closet and mimic his posture. "I've spent two dozen years scandalizing my family and friends; they're pretty inured to it. But your family . . ." I open my hands in supplication. "I want them to like me."

He crosses the room and pulls me into a hug. "They will. And you don't have to hide the bruises if you don't want to."

"I'm twenty years older than you. They're going to think I'm a middle-aged pervert taking advantage of their young son." I flush as I say it, this sudden lack of confidence making my voice shake.

"So what? Middle-aged perverts are my *favorite*." He affects my lilt, then he gets serious. "I like you the way you are. My family will too. You aren't the first older guy I've dated, you know."

"I'm probably closer to your mother's age than to yours." I huff, reaching for the lacing on my shorts as he returns to the bathroom.

"You are."

"And she's not going to mind?"

"I don't let my mom pick my boyfriends for me. Wear whatever you like. I think you're perfect."

And then he turns on the shower and the conversation is over.

I wear the green Speedo but pull my Nantucket Reds over it. At least until we get the introductions out of the way.

Wish's family is meeting us at the marina, which is good because I feel much less self-conscious about it than about my house. The cabin cruiser is already pulled into my boat slip, and our lunch is packed on ice in the little galley, along with a bottle of champagne, some Cokes and bottled waters, and a twelve pack of fancy microbrew. I don't know much about either wine or beer, but I figure things are expensive because they're good, so I bought the fancy shit. I hope Wish doesn't know any more about these things than I do, because then I'm totally busted trying to impress his family.

The boat was cleaned and detailed after the last time I used it—I prefer the wake boat because the cruiser uses an insane amount of fuel and isn't practical. But it is the best way to see the tournament from the lake—comfortable and luxurious.

Wish stands at the bottom of the stairs to the cabin and turns in a circle while I watch him from above. "We are *so* sleeping here tonight." He points at the bed. "That is . . . There's a bedroom on your boat."

"It's more like a cupboard." I shrug. "But if you want to, we can sleep in it."

"Sleep is a euphemism." He winks at me, and I flush warm all over. "Wow." He spins around again. "Max is gonna shit."

"Well, I guess it's a good thing there's a toilet too." I gesture up the stairs. "Come on, help me watch for your family."

It turns out, I wouldn't have needed help. His brother, though taller and a little broader, is nearly identical to Wish. Same blue eyes and brown hair. Same blinding smile.

"This is my brother, Max, and his wife, Carrie," Wish introduces. "And this is my mom, Kelly Carver." He grins as he helps his mom onto the deck.

She can't be a day over fifty. Her dark hair is still short, growing in from the chemo, making her bright-blue eyes appear huge in her thin face. She's wearing a red sundress and carrying a broad black-and-white hat.

"It's lovely to meet you all," I say, glancing at Wish and his big, reassuring smile. "Wish has told me a lot about you."

"Don't believe a word," Max groans.

"Aloysius said you were older, but he didn't mention how handsome you were." Kelly smiles at me. "He probably thought I'd try to steal you away."

"Mom." Wish covers his face with one hand and shakes his head, gesturing at me with the other. "Gay!"

"All the ones who can still find their abs at forty-five are, sweetheart. And if we're going to be dating guys in the same age group, I get to harass you about it."

Wish throws his arm around her shoulders, clearly comfortable with the teasing. He gives me a coy little smile as if to say, "See, I *told* you."

"Edward!" Mom's panicked voice calls from behind me just before Ricochet comes leaping onto the deck, leash dangling behind him. I grab the leash and pull him up short before he can jump on my guests, and then I scoop him up and turn around.

"Hi, Mama."

"I'm sorry, Ed. He saw you and took off." She flaps her hands as I reach to help her onto the boat, preferring to find her own footing. I introduce her to Wish's family and ask her to take the wheel as I glance at my watch; Tina is late. I scan the docks for any sign of Elvis's sparkly leash and collar.

I worry about Tina. Not in the same way I worry about Ben— she's never seemed quite as fragile—but in a big-brother way. When she isn't where she says she'll be, I get nervous.

"I don't know anyone who still wears a watch," Max says, pointing at my wrist. "Doesn't everyone use their phone?"

"Heirlooms and habits are hard to abandon." I peek down at my wrist again. The watch is worth almost as much as the boat, but I see no point in mentioning that. "It reminds me of my father."

Wish comes up behind me and wraps an arm around my waist. "Why don't you call her?"

But as I'm taking my phone out, she comes sprinting up the dock toward my slip, Elvis nowhere in sight.

"Sorry I'm late. Is everyone here already?"

"It's about time." I roll my eyes to cover my relief. "And yes, everyone is here except you and Elvis. Where's the mutt?"

"He's with Joe." She shrugs, then bends down to untie the boat from the dock. She tosses me the rope and explains, "She has a summer cold, and I left him with her to cheer her up."

"And who, Tina-cakes, is Joe?" I move the bumpers inside as she unties the last rope. She pulls the boat closer with it, then hops across, taking my hand.

"Joe is a new friend." She grins at me. "And she is way cuter than Ben."

Well. Good for *her.*

I pack away the bumpers and ropes and offer to take the wheel from Mama, but she waves me off.

"I'm fine, honey. Catch up with your friends."

I turn to see Tina stripping down to her bikini. A huge green and purple bruise covers her leg from knee to hip.

"What the hell happened to you?" I blurt out.

She glances down at her leg and grins. "Nasty fall. Not a serious one though."

"It sure as hell looks serious." I'm familiar with bruises, and this one speaks of impact that could break bones. "And what are you grinning about?"

"You know how, when you meet someone, and you get all wrapped up in them, giddy at the thought of them, and the time you spend with them seems brighter and more intense than anything else in your life?"

I can't help it; I sneak a glance at Wish, who's moved to sit next to his mom. His hair is flapping in the breeze, and he's pulled his T-shirt off so he can put sunscreen on his shoulders. He's smiling at his mom and when he catches my gaze, his smile gets bigger.

"Yeah, I know what you mean." I turn my attention back to her. "So, you feel that way about this Joe?"

She laughs. "Nope. I feel that way about *derby*."

"Derby? Like, roller derby?"

"Yep." She pokes my abs with a finger. "You should come see our next bout."

The mind boggles. I didn't even know Lake Lovelace had a roller derby team, let alone that Tina was on it. I really have been wrapped up in Wish.

"I can do that. Send me the details, and Wish and I will make a date of it."

"I saw you look at him just then," she singsongs.

"So what?" I glare at her.

"Nothing. Not saying a word." She holds up her hands. "Put some sunscreen on my back, okay?"

We pull the cruiser up to the spectator area early enough to get a prime watching spot, and we put the bumpers out and tie up to a wake boat on one side. We'll be blocked in from behind soon, but that's par for the course for events on the lake. Tina, Wish, and I sit up above the bow while the rest of the group watches from the sundeck.

We can hear Ben's voice rumbling through the speakers, but only barely.

"God, I hope the script banter is better than last year's." Tina rolls her eyes. "I don't know how he and the beauty queen kept a straight face."

"Eh, they're professionals. That's what they do." I shrug, watching Wish watch the riders.

He turns to Tina and asks, "Where are the girls?"

"They ride tomorrow. Too big a tournament to do it all in one day."

He nods. "You riding tomorrow?"

She shakes her head. "Nah. I thought I might, but I've been busy with other things and I'm out of practice."

"But you used to ride pro, right? Like Ben? Surely muscle memory and whatnot . . ."

She laughs. "Baby, that was years ago. And I'm . . ." She looks up at me, a question in her eyes. I shake my head to indicate I haven't told Wish she's trans. I figure it's up to her how much she wants to tell. "My body has changed a lot. I was assigned male at birth, and lived as a man until I was in my twenties. My center of balance is different. My muscles are different. I need to train *this* body all over again if I want to really compete."

He stares blankly at her for a moment, then nods. "Yeah. I can see how that would . . . I'm sorry . . . I pried for real personal info, didn't I?"

She shrugs. "No biggie."

He smiles at her, and I feel something in me relax. Relief—not that I thought he'd freak out, but I've seen all kinds of reactions to people learning Tina is trans, and some of them were ugly. His is reassuring. One more assurance he's the guy I think he is. One more realization that for all his youth, he's much more of a grown-up than I ever was at his age.

"Okay, so tell me who I need to watch. Who are the superstars? Underdogs?" He gestures toward the competition area.

"You really want to watch Dave's little brother, Ridley," Tina says. "The kid is insane. He'll ride in the pro group. In the advanced group, keep an eye on Ridley's friend Caden. I don't know anyone in the intermediate or beginner groups, but those two guys are the big local attraction this year."

I close my eyes and soak up the sunshine as she explains the way the tournament works. Occasionally I take in snippets of Ben's banter with his co-emcee this year, and I try not to laugh at the way he's deliberately masking his accent. Somehow, I doze off, only startling awake when something cold drips on my belly.

"Beer?" Max holds the bottle out to me. I glance at my watch. We'll be here for hours yet. I nod, and he twists the cap off for me, then hands one to his brother.

"Who's winning?" I ask, winking at Tina.

"An eight-year-old kid won the beginner group. Jesus. They get younger every year." She shakes her head. "I don't know the guy who won the intermediate group. Oh, hey, advanced group is up next."

I take a long pull on my beer, and tug Wish closer. He lets me drag him into a kiss, then gives me a nip of teeth on my lip.

"Gonna start calling you 'Sleeping Beauty,'" he teases. "I can't believe you can sleep with all this noise around you."

I snort. "It's the sunshine, and rocking on the water. It's like a drug."

To prove my point, I close my eyes again, but he presses his cold beer against my side, and I yelp and sit up straight.

"Sadist," I grumble, wiping my ribs with his discarded T-shirt.

"It's why you love me." He shrugs, then touches the beer to my chest, right over my heart.

Love. Is that what I feel for him? This giddy affection, this spiral of lust and comfort, tempered by longing and fear? If it's love, and I have a sneaking suspicion it's starting to be, it isn't because he's a sadist. Sure, that's *nice* and really *convenient*, but it's not what makes my breath catch when I see him.

"No." I grab the bottle and look him straight in the eye. "It really isn't."

The teasing smile on his face softens, and he leans in and kisses me, a sensual assault of tenderness and roughness together that ramps me up. I pull back and duck my head, suddenly conscious of our families all here in the boat with us.

"It's not why for me, either," he says in a whisper so quiet, I'd think I imagined it, but then his arm comes around my shoulders and he points with his other hand toward the competition. "Let's watch."

chapter TEN

that evening, we say good-bye to our families and Tina at the docks, exchanging sunscreen-laced hugs and heartfelt "See ya later"s. But I'm itching to get Wish alone.

"Did you mean it, about sleeping out on the water?" I ask.

"Can we? I don't have a change of clothes, but maybe we can swing by your house from the lakeside?"

"Or we can dock up there in the morning." I untie us and gesture for him to take the wheel as I tuck the ropes away. "We can anchor over by the park campgrounds. It's quiet out there at night, even on a holiday weekend. Or we can anchor by my place, in case we change our minds about that tiny bed."

"The park sounds really nice. Tiny bed means sleeping closer to you."

He makes me smile, a completely wild, unself-conscious smile. And he has no idea what a gift he gives me every time. I'm a guy who calculates each emotion I let cross my face. But tonight, with him, I don't care if he sees my feelings as they happen. I'm not afraid, or trying to jockey for position. I'm here, with him, and free.

"You should smile like that more often," he says, slowing us to a stop. "I don't know where the park is; you'll have to drive."

But he doesn't move out of the captain's chair, so I sit on his lap.

He wraps an arm around my waist and widens his legs to cradle me comfortably. "So, S-Class. We need to talk about this." He runs a finger over the bite mark on my shoulder, drawing a shiver from me.

"What about it?"

"I broke the skin. There was blood."

I shrug. "I told you, it was hot. It didn't bother me."

"I got that. But if our play is getting rough like—I mean, if there's blood involved—we should talk about precautions."

Oh. *Oh.*

"I've tested negative for everything you can possibly be tested for. As far as I know, that bit of blood you tasted is harmless."

"Okay, I'm negative too. I mean, I haven't had sex without a condom since I moved here, and I tested negative at my last physical. I had Tommy's blood all over me on Monday, so I should probably get tested again, but after . . ."

"Are you asking if we can start barebacking?" I tease, glancing at him over my shoulder.

He blushes. "I'm asking if we're monogamous."

I let go of the wheel with one hand and grip his hand in my own. "I haven't been seeing anyone else since the day I ran my car off the highway. I'm all yours if that's what you want."

"It's what I want." He presses a kiss onto my shoulder, then bites softly. "It's definitely what I want. Is it what you want?"

I lay my head back against his shoulder as I steer us into the wide cove where the campground sits. A few fires dot the shoreline, and the beach is crowded, but I choose an anchorage far enough away that only the loudest shouts reach our ears. We slow to a stop, and I turn so I can look him in the eye while I say it.

"I want you. And I want you to be happy. If you want us to be monogamous, I'm all for it. If you wanted to play with someone else, say at Keith's? I'd want to talk about it first, and I'd expect you to be safe. But I'm okay with letting you set the boundaries here."

"What if you wanted to play with someone else? Like that night with Keith?" He tenses, his blue eyes dark in the fading sunlight.

"Oh." I glance down and see our hands clasped together. "I don't think I want that. But if you wanted me to—"

"I don't." He laughs. "It was hot, watching you with Keith. But it was different, we weren't . . . we weren't *us* yet. I think I'd feel differently now."

"I feel differently now." I squeeze his hand.

He swallows, then squeezes back. "Let's put the anchor out and go downstairs."

I grin. "I've never actually had sex on this boat before."

He helps me drop anchor, and we head into the cabin. He stops halfway down the stairs and turns to me. "I just had a thought. I could . . . I could call Tommy."

"Your friend with the leg? Why— Oh." A shudder runs through me.

"I mean, it's gonna be a hella awkward conversation, but worth it if it means we don't have to wait six months for the all clear."

"Well, this should be interesting." I'm trying to imagine how this conversation can play out, and any way I picture it is humiliating. At least Tommy will be on medical leave and Wish won't have to see him for a while.

He pulls his phone from his pocket and dials. His hand is shaking. My poor lovely.

"Hey, Tommy, how ya feeling?"

He listens to the voice on the other end for a minute, a sad smile forming on his lips. "Yeah, I broke my arm when I was a kid. The itching, man." His face flushes. "Oh, well, you're welcome. That's actually why I was calling, you see . . . I didn't have . . . um, I mean I didn't . . ."

Oh dear.

I snag the phone from him.

"Hello, Thomas?" I lay the lilt on extra heavy. "This is Edward Russell, Wish's boyfriend."

"Um, hi?" Tommy's voice is confused, but I roll ahead anyway.

"Listen, Wish is concerned about the exchange of fluids. He got quite a bit of your blood on him the other day, and he wasn't wearing any protective gear. We have a bit of a romantic evening planned, and he—and I, let's be honest—need to know if he needs to take any precautions before we, ahem, engage?"

Silence. Wish's eyes have gone wide.

"Hellooooo?" I trill a little on the *o*. If you don't go all out, don't go out at all. "Thomas? Are you there?"

"Oh man." I can practically hear him cringing on the other end of the line. "Did you call me—in my hospital room—to ask if you can fuck your boyfriend without a condom?"

"And they say painkillers dull the mind!"

"Am I being punked?"

"Focus, Thomas. It's a yes-or-no question."

"No, dude. No. You don't have anything to worry about."

"Thank you, dear heart. Heal up quick, now." I hang up the phone and catch Wish's mortified expression.

"I cannot believe you did that, like *that*."

"I excel at awkward conversations. It comes with being shameless. Now, let's get you out of these trunks." I reach for the laces on his board shorts.

"You really are shameless, aren't you?" He stills my hands on his trunks and moves them behind my back, not forcefully, but gently, like he's testing me.

I nod, letting the smile spread on my face, and I try to tug my hands out of his grasp. He tightens it, careful not to tip me off-balance here on the stairwell.

"I like you shameless." He pushes me back against the bulkhead and kisses me. It's a sensual, unhurried kiss, roughness hinted at under the lazy sweep of his tongue against mine and in the steady grip of my wrists in his hand. I thrust my hips against his, and he rewards me with a slow, steady grind and a bite to my lip. His lips travel across my cheekbone, featherlight, then he catches my ear between his teeth, a sharp pinch of pain.

"Bed now?" he whispers, then soothes my ear with a tickling kiss.

"Yeah." I rock against him again, and he lets go of my wrists and grabs me around the waist. *So strong.* I wrap my legs around him as he carries me the rest of the way down the stairs, through the tiny galley to dump me on the bed beyond.

Out the portholes on one side, I see the flicker of fires on the beach, from the other I see nothing but starlight.

The cruiser rocks with the wake of a passing boat as I peel off my Speedo and Wish sheds his trunks. He lands on the bed on top of me with an enthusiastic *thump*, wrapping his arms around me to pull me close. I feel his erection push against my thigh, and I wriggle and turn until I can take it in my mouth, thrusting my own against his shoulder in a none-too-subtle hint.

I taste the lake on him, mixed with his salty sweat and the tang of pre-cum. It's a heady taste, the combination of this man and this place.

Home. I tremble as he takes me in hand and pumps me slowly. He tugs at the Prince Albert, sending a shivery sensation down my cock.

"Wish I could have seen you get this done," he murmurs against it, then licks a line from one end of the barbell around to the other. "Would love to see your reaction to the needle going in. Goddamn."

The idea of him watching a needle pierce my body shoots through me like wildfire, stealing my breath. I gasp around his cock, then suck him harder as his hand finds my balls and the ring behind them. He gives that one a tug as his mouth engulfs me, and I let go of his cock to groan against his thigh.

We tease like that, building the heat between us, until we're rocking desperately into each other's mouths. Then, he pulls off and leaves me twisting on the edge, urgency boiling up in me, but not tipping over. I let go of his cock and shift onto my hands and knees next to him. I look over my shoulder at him and beg, "Fuck me."

He sits up and reaches for my legs, pushing them farther apart. He slaps one cheek, then the other, not hard enough to really even sting, raising a prickly warmth. He moves up over me quickly, shoving my face down to the bed. My arms buckle underneath me, and I fall forward, my ass still in the air. The force in his touch sings to me, and I settle into the bed as he grabs my wrists and holds them at the small of my back.

"Don't move," he orders, letting go and heading for the stairs.

Yeah, right. I roll onto my side and pillow my head with my arm. I'm not feeling quite rebellious enough to follow him to the deck naked, but I do watch his ass all the way up the steps.

When he comes back holding thick marine ropes, I can't help the grin or the flutter of excitement in my chest.

"I told you to stay put," he growls, a playful light in his eye.

"Fuck off." I flip him the bird.

He pounces.

Looming over me on the bed, he grabs for my wrists. I struggle, bringing my knees up against his thigh. We grapple for control, but with him, a trained wrestler, on top, there's not much I can do, and when he pins my thighs apart with his own legs, I sink back to the bed in acquiescence.

"I'm going to tie your wrists behind your back. I'm going to play with your ass, maybe spank it, maybe paddle it. Maybe fuck it. Maybe hold you open and stare at it."

The wash of humiliation at his words makes my body hum.

"You want that, Eddie?"

I shake my head. "Just shut up and fuck me."

He laughs, then rolls me over, tying my hands like he said he would. The polyester fiber of the rope is scratchy, not designed for human comfort, but to resist decay in wet environments. Its roughness is going to leave marks, and that turns me on even more than if he'd restrained me with the nicest silk ropes.

He shoves my knees under me so my ass sticks up, then takes another rope and loops it from my wrists to my ankles and back, securing me in position, taking care to leave my genitals hanging free between my legs. I have enough slack to spread my legs farther, and could probably get my ankles free if I really worked at it, but now I'm too turned on to try.

I feel a finger at my hole, nudging insistently inside. He groans, low and loud in the dark cabin.

"You're so tight and hot. Gonna feel so good to slide inside you bare. Can't wait to see you push my cum out of this hot little hole." He pulls his finger back and flicks my guiche ring. I squirm, straining against the ropes binding my wrists.

"I brought something for you," he whispers. "I had it in my bag all day, waiting for everyone else to go home. I got hard just thinking about using it."

He reaches behind him, then puts something on the bed in my field of vision. My favorite paddle, only about an inch wide, with soft leather on one side and smooth, polished wood on the other. The smell of leather invades my senses before he takes it away, using it to draw a line down the center of my back, tiptoeing along each vertebra until he reaches my crack. He slides it along the cleft of my ass, leather and wood warming to my skin. I wriggle back, begging for something with my body, anticipating the whistle of it through the air, the soft thud against my skin, the sharp sting.

"Please," I whisper. "Want it."

And he gives it to me. The whistle, the thud, the bright, bright burst of delicious pain across both cheeks. I feel my flesh lift as the paddle moves up slightly, then releases me.

Another crack, two, three. He stops every so often to play with my balls and tease my guiche ring, but leaves my cock hanging hard and heavy between my legs. The deprivation there makes me squirm and arch into his next swing.

"You have stripes on your ass. They won't last as long as the ones from the caning, but you won't be able to sit down without knowing I did this." He grunts as he strikes me again, letting fly. He knows how much I can take.

Tears sting my eyes, but it feels pulse-poundingly good. The next strike makes me cry out, and then his hand is there, rubbing the stinging flesh, squeezing it and soothing.

"Fuck me," I demand.

He groans, grabbing my hips and rolling his dick against my ass. "Wanted to get you more worked up first, but I don't think I can wait."

"I'm worked up, trust me. Want to feel you lose it."

"Lube?" he asks, and I gesture toward the little drawers built into the bulkhead by the bed. I hear the drawer open and close, the click of the bottle, and the wet sound of lube on skin.

He rubs two fingers over my hole, pressing a fingertip inside to lube me up. I push back, asking for more. He adds more lube, working it into me, and then replaces his hand with his dick.

Bare.

The intimacy of trusting him with my body enough to say he can have me like this, and no one else can, makes the moment enormous and pivotal, eclipsing anything we'd done before.

He pushes in slowly, a deep, constant pressure, and I rut backward, trying to take him faster, wanting to feel every inch of him, hot and naked inside me.

His hand comes down on my ass with a loud slap, right over the paddle marks. "I'm setting the pace."

With my hands behind my back and my face chafing against the comforter, there's nothing I can do but let him. At this angle, he feels huge—and the slide of his skin, the friction and the heat of his body? Delicious.

"You feel so good," he says, a tremor to his voice. "So hot."

He sinks in the rest of the way, his balls slapping forward, and we both groan. His arms come down and wrap around me, pressing my back to his chest, my bound hands caught between us. His lips find the nape of my neck, and he brushes tender kisses there. I rock a little, and he lets me set the rhythm now, a small gasp slipping from his lips.

He starts to fuck into me harder, and I need a hand on my dick. I struggle against the ropes, and he lifts off me, dragging me back with one hand on my hip to keep himself inside me. He reaches around and grabs my dick.

"Come on, honey. Come on."

The gentle words, the roughness of his motions, the harsh gasps of his breath and the heat of the summer air. So much sensation.

"Bite me," I demand, and he does, right on my shoulder, then he groans, loud, and thrusts into me harder.

I revel in that violence, let it take over my body as I shove back against my bonds, against him, while he ruts into me faster. My orgasm hits almost without warning, and there's only time to shout, "Please!" and to shudder helplessly in his hands while my dick shoots across the bedcovers.

He cries out a moment later, then stills—I feel the heat of him coming inside me, and I shudder again, excited and sated together. His hand makes small circles on my back, his breath slowing. He eases out of me, and I grunt at the loss of him. Then he's untying me, rubbing my arms and legs and helping me to my shaky feet.

He makes sure I'm steady enough, then he leads me to the sink in the galley, turns it on, and grabs a small dishtowel from the cupboard. He cleans me up, pausing to play with my ass, fingering me and groaning at the slide of his cum around my hole.

"God, this is hot." He sounds breathless, and I don't blame him; it turns me on too. He teases me a moment longer, until I'm moaning, and then finishes cleaning me and inspects the marks on my ass.

"You're gonna bruise a little," he gloats.

"I don't care." I shrug, and the motion almost tips me over.

"Bedtime." He leads me back to bed, helps me climb in, and then slides beneath the covers and pulls me close. A warm contentment steals over me, and I roll my head into his shoulder as I rub my stinging ass against the sheets.

chapter ELEVEN

the next few weeks are almost perfect, but one thing niggles in the back of my mind. It bothers me more than I'd like to admit that he hasn't invited me to hang out with him and his friends. It's not that I'm just dying to spend time with a group of guys half my age, but we've been dating long enough that I'm starting to feel like he's hiding me from them. Oh yeah, he *said* he didn't care about me being all over the top, but he hasn't exactly proven that to me. When I'm over at his apartment and I overhear him making plans—without me—for the last weekend in September, I decide to do something about it.

"Are you ashamed of me?" I ask as he hangs up the phone and picks up his Xbox controller.

"What? No. Of course not. Why would you think that?" He glances at me, then back at the TV screen.

"Please pause the game for me, lovely."

He looks over at me again, obviously realizes I'm serious, and sets the controller down. "What's up? Why would you think I'm ashamed of you?"

"Because for at least the third time this month, you've accepted an invitation to a social engagement without even asking if you could bring me along."

"I didn't invite you to Greg's softball thing because you hate sports. And that work picnic was totally boring."

"Do the other guys bring their girlfriends and wives?"

He shrugs. "I guess so. I never really thought about it. I mean, if you want to go next year, that's cool."

How optimistic of him. I pinch the skin at the top of my nose between two fingers and take a deep breath.

"And this weekend, you're going where?"

"A bunch of the guys from work and I are going over to Tommy's house to help out with some yard work he can't do because of his leg. Then we're having a barbecue. I didn't think you'd want to come along."

"I love barbecue." I arch an eyebrow.

"But it's work—yard work."

"A bunch of strapping young men with their shirts off, hauling heavy things and getting dirty: I don't know what could possibly be appealing about that."

"You'd really want to come?"

"I really want to get to know your friends. Is that so odd? I mean, you've met Ben and Tina and everyone."

"Okay, hold on." He digs in his pocket and pulls out his phone. He dials, then, "Hey, Greg? Yeah, got another pair of hands for the landscaping thing. No, not Jordan. Eddie, my boyfriend." He winks at me. "Yeah, okay, we'll see you then."

"Thank you," I say quietly as he hangs up.

"You're welcome." He reaches for his controller.

"So, this game, does it have a two-player option?" I ask.

"Yard work and video games? Who are you and what have you done with my boyfriend?" He leans over and kisses me. "I'm sorry, from now on I won't assume you wouldn't want to do something. I'll ask first."

Okay, so I've never actually done yard work before. And Wish knows this, and who knows what he's expecting? Probably for me to make some grand faux pas—is there even an etiquette to yard work? I can't help but have a little fun.

I go to the Ace Hardware, and I buy gloves and coveralls—and some rope too, but that's for later—and the guy at Ace Hardware tells me to go buy some steel-toe Red Wings, so I've got those too—they might be overkill, or they might be the only useful thing in the whole mess. When Wish picks me up at 7 a.m. on Saturday, I'm ready to go.

His reaction is priceless—absolutely horrified.

"What?" I snap, looking down at my coveralls. "They're green— *my color.*"

"Oh, honey, you can't wear those in September in Florida. You'll die of heat stroke."

I make my face as crestfallen as possible. "Well, come on in, I'll go change."

"Just wear whatever you have underneath them."

I turn and give him a *look.* "I'm not wearing anything underneath them."

I think that's the moment he realizes he's been played, because he howls with laughter.

"Well, they never have anything on underneath them in *porn,*" I shout, peeling the coveralls off as I go.

I change into khaki shorts and a plain white undershirt, and meet him back downstairs. He's stopped laughing and actually appears contrite.

"I'm sorry I underestimated you." He kisses my cheek. "We can play porno later."

"Oh goody, I bought rope too."

Tommy seems to have forgiven me for what had to be the most awkward phone call he's ever received. He only blushes a little when he opens the door.

"Nice ride." Wish takes in the chair with a glance. "Can you do wheelies in that thing?"

"Doctor says no way, but the orderlies told me it's totally possible. You wanna try it?"

"Maybe after we finish up outside. I won't be much good to you guys if I bust my leg and end up needing one too."

The work is hard. Intense, sweaty, back-breaking labor. By 9 a.m. I've stripped off my shirt, and by lunchtime I'm wishing I had picked another weekend to get to know Wish's friends.

But I like them.

Greg Conlon, the foreman from his road crew, is smart and organized. He has the group of volunteer landscapers moving around like the many pieces of a well-oiled machine. They're all younger than me, but they tease me about it which makes me feel like one of them rather than an outsider. It's not a weekend on the boat with Ben and Dave or Tina, but it's a different type of easy camaraderie, and something about manual labor appeals to my masochist streak.

"Nice work, old man." Greg walks past the row of pavers I've painstakingly aligned with the lanai, and he swats my ass as he goes by.

"You flirting with my boyfriend, Conlon?" Wish shouts from across the yard, where he's been digging around a cactus to transplant.

"Hey, he might want to trade up." The foreman holds his hands out and preens, showing off a hairy barrel chest dripping with sweat.

I shake my head. "Dear God in heaven, save me from open-minded straight boys."

They all laugh, and then I go to help Wish move the cactus and chance a kiss.

At the end of the day, after the work and the barbecue, Greg looks me right in the eye and holds out a hand.

"I gotta be honest, when I heard Wish was bringing the guy from the radio who's trying to defeat the roads bill, I thought you'd be a real asshole. But you're all right."

I shake the offered hand. "Thank you, I think. No hard feelings about the roads thing?"

"Only if you win." He winks.

Fair enough, I suppose.

At home, my muscles aching from the day's labor, I grab the rope, put on the coveralls, and go find Wish in the bedroom. His eyes light up and he drags me down to the bed and kisses me until I'm hard and breathless.

"I'm not going to say what I thought when I opened the door and saw you in these," he says as he pulls out of the kiss. "But you got me good, and I deserved it. You are seriously amazing."

"Mm-hmm." I bite his ear. "Thanks for letting me tag along; it was fun."

He reaches for the first snap at the top of the coveralls and pauses. "You didn't buy the kind with a zipper."

"Nope." I laugh.

He leaves me buttoned, runs his hands down my body, hard. It feels good on my sore muscles, and I arch up into those hands.

He flips me over and starts working my shoulders through the coveralls, a nice, hard rub. I melt into it and relax under his touch. When he rolls me back over, my dick is the only part of my body that's still stiff. He undoes the snap right over my groin, freeing my cock so it pokes up out of the coveralls.

"God, that is—" he gives it a good firm stroke "—the best kind of obscene."

I thrust into his hand a little and bite my lip, relaxed, aroused, ready to come out of my skin—

And the phone rings. The Dead Kennedys. Only one person in my address book has an eighties punk ringtone.

"Hold that thought, lovely." I grab the phone and his eyes go wide with disbelief.

"You're not seriously going to answer that now."

"I *have* to." I swipe to answer.

"Ben, can I call you back, darling?"

Wish stands up. "Don't bother. I've lost the mood." And just like that he strides out of the room.

"And you're seriously walking away again?" I call after him.

"Sorry, did I interrupt something?" Ben asks.

"Apparently not." The sudden change of plans has my dick deflating back into my coveralls like it's trying to flee the scene.

"I need to know how to spell your dude's name. We're addressing wedding invitations."

I resist the petulant urge to tell the big fucking cockblocker about Google. "A-l-o-y-s-i-u-s."

"Awesome. Thanks, man. You coming by the shop Monday?"

Month-close books. Of course. "Yeah, I'll be there."

"See you then."

"See ya."

I find Wish in the living room, fully clothed and pissed off, watching something on the television with lots of explosions.

"So, want to test out the rope?" I try my most flirtatious voice.

"Really not in the mood anymore."

"Okay. Do you want to talk about it?"

He snorts. "I really, really don't."

"I asked him if I could call him back. I wasn't planning to have a conversation with him." I cross my arms over my chest and glare at him. I don't know why I feel the need to defend myself here, but for some reason I do.

He groans and covers his face with both hands. "I am not going to fight with you."

"I don't want to fight either. Come to bed."

"I think I'd like to watch this movie. Daniel Craig is my favorite Bond."

"Oooh, he's fucking hot. Well, let's watch, then." I go back to the bedroom and change out of the coveralls and into my robe, then join him on the couch. At first he flinches away a little when I move in for the snuggle, but then he relaxes and lets me. I fall asleep with my head on his shoulder, and when he wakes me up as the credits are rolling, he isn't pissed anymore.

"Let's go get some sleep, Eddie."

chapter TWELVE

The envelope, when it arrives in the middle of October, is bigger than the usual bills and advertisements that land in my mailbox, but I don't register why until I rip it open and pull out the wedding invitation.

It's a simple thing: Two names, an expression of joy. A date at the end of November and the address of a hotel in Charleston, South Carolina.

I sit down heavily in the kitchen and stare at it for a while. I knew it was coming, but it's still taken me by surprise. I trace the words with my fingers, as if feeling their texture will help me understand my own confused longings for what this paper represents. *Benjamin Warren and Davis Fox . . .*

"Eddie?" Wish calls out as he opens the front door.

"Kitchen," I shout, shoving the invitation back in the envelope and pushing it away, schooling my face.

"Hey." He walks in, all smiles, with a grocery bag in hand. He comes to the table first and bends over to kiss me deep and slow, then sets the bag on the counter and starts rummaging through it. "I thought we could make carne asada tomorrow, but it's got to marinate overnight. What's that?" He gestures to the envelope.

"Ben's wedding invitation."

"Oh." He stops rummaging and comes to sit at the table. He stares at me for a moment and then picks up the envelope, pulls out the invitation, and reads it over. "I've never been to Charleston."

"It's old," I mutter, "and pretty."

"So, that explains the pity party." His voice is cold and flat, and when I glance up at him, his gaze is equally so.

"Excuse me?"

"Come on, Eddie. I *know* you. You're working so hard right now to turn your face to stone."

"I have no idea what you mean." I can't meet his eyes as I say it.

"You finally realized at some point in the last year that the guy you're carrying a torch for isn't ever going to love you the way you want him to. I figured—at least I hoped—you'd get over it eventually, especially after we've been so—" He swallows and looks away, the stark vulnerability on his face breaking my heart as much as his words piss me off. "Apparently not."

"You don't understand. It's not like that." How can I explain twenty-something years of *Ben* to a twenty-four-year-old without sounding like he's not old enough to get it?

"The fuck it isn't. It's exactly like that. You would move mountains for that man. You keep a room for him in your house. You turn down pain medicine after a car accident. You answer the phone no matter what time of day or night he's calling, no matter what you're doing, and no matter *who* you're doing it with. He's in love with someone else. And even when you congratulate him on his upcoming wedding, you're still calculating how *you* can be better *for him.*"

The vehemence in his final words stuns me for a moment, and I stare at him, mouth opening and closing like a fish.

"That's . . ." I gasp, pain flaring in my chest, sudden and sharp. "It's *not like that.*"

"Eddie. I can love you when you're being self-absorbed. I can love you when you're mouthing off to me to try and get me to spank you harder. I can love you when you're distracted by work or town politics or what have you. But I can't love your insistence on martyring yourself for this guy. I get it: he's your best friend and you're absolutely fucking blind with love for him. But it's killing me to see it and wonder what it would take to get you to care like that about me."

"I care about you." *Love. He said love. And he said it a lot.*

"Not enough to move a mountain. Not even enough to move a boat dealership."

"This tantrum is about the *roads project?*"

He throws his hands up in the air. "Let's face it, that's the real reason you're opposed to it. You're protecting Ben. Because he always comes first for you. Even when you're both with other people. He comes first."

"He's *family*."

It's *totally* the wrong thing to say. I know it the moment it comes out of my mouth. His face gets harder, turns red, his eyebrows drawing together.

"And I'm just a regular source of kinky sex."

"Now you're putting words into my mouth," I protest. "It hasn't been just sex between us since that night at Keith's club, and you know it."

"I wish I did. I really want to believe that—"

My phone ringing cuts him off. The Dead Kennedys. I reach to pick it up, and he covers my hand with his own, his face and voice pleading.

"Don't answer it. Let us have this conversation without *him* interrupting."

But my mind flashes back to a night years ago when Tina called me from Ben's phone in a panic because she found him passed out and couldn't wake him.

"I *have* to." I start to lift the phone, and he holds my hand down. "Do you *mind*?" I snarl, wrenching my hand out of his grasp.

"Hey, Ben, can I . . ." I drop my hand as Wish shoves away from the table, knocking his chair over.

"I'm done, Eddie. I can't do this anymore." The vulnerable expression is gone, his features crumpled in defeat. My stomach sinks.

"Wish, wait!"

"No. You keep choosing *him*. I won't sit around and be your second choice. I deserve to be someone's first choice." He shakes his head and walks out of the kitchen. The front door slams and the realization hits me. I proved his point—he's gone. And it's my fault.

I put the phone back to my ear.

"Darling, I've fucked up. We need to talk."

"How bad?" His voice is gruff across the phone line.

I stare at the chair tipped on its side and remember the way Wish's face fell and his eyes got bright and glassy.

"Bad."

"Come on over."

Ben greets me at the door of his house with a somber expression. I know Ben better than I know anyone else in my life, but that expression is one I don't recognize. There's none of the deep desperation of his years fighting addiction. There's none of the Peter Pan–like joy he exhibits behind a boat. He's just . . . calm and sad. A part of me wants to fling myself into his arms and fall apart, to let him pick up the pieces the way I always have for him. Another, sharper, part of me wants to pick a fight, to *make* him take some responsibility for our codependent relationship. But I can't do either of those things.

"Come on in." He pushes the door wide. "Dave went out."

"Out?"

"Out. To give us privacy."

"Oh." I send out a mental *thank you* to Dave, and follow Ben into the house—as familiar to me as my own. He flicks on a light with a remote control and we settle down on the sofa. It's a far cry from the dark apartment where we had our last come-to-Jesus talk.

"Is this about the wedding invitation?" he asks, his normally gruff voice gentle.

"Only tangentially." I can't let Ben take the blame, so I choose my words carefully. My voice still shakes. "Wish showed up right after I got it, and he said some things. And then my phone rang—"

"Ah, Christ, Eddie. You have *got* to stop doing that. I can leave you a voice mail."

Oh, now *that* stings.

"But what if it's an emergency? What if you needed me?"

He digs the heel of his hand into his eyes, then squints at me. "Who would you call? If you had an emergency? If something happened to you tomorrow, who would be your first call?"

I don't even have to think about it. "Wish."

"And my first call is to Dave."

See, I *know* that. I know it, but a part of me still wants to protest it. "But what if you can't reach him? What if he's on a plane, or at a remote jobsite? And then I don't answer?"

"Then I'll call Tina, or I can call Wish looking for you, or Jerry. I'll keep calling until I get someone. But you don't have to be my knight in shining armor. It's okay to let my calls go."

"Wish thinks I'm in love with you."

"Dave thinks you are too."

I stare at him, and he holds my gaze. How can they be right and still be so wrong?

"I do love you." I break the eye contact and start tracing a pattern on the sofa. "You're my best friend. And I love you. And I think that's normal. I don't think I love you in a way that isn't normal for friends."

"What the fuck does that even mean?"

"I don't want to be with you. I don't want to have sex with you. I don't want to marry you. My feelings for you are more . . . protective?"

"Controlling." He snorts, and I laugh, but sober quickly.

"I like being there for you."

"And I like knowing you're there—but I want you to have your own life too."

"So you really don't need me anymore? You're the only person in my life who has ever needed me."

He steeples his fingers under his chin and frowns at me. "I still need you. I just don't need . . . I don't need you to take care of me. I don't need you to be on call for me twenty-four hours a day. I am never not going to need my best friend to be a huge part of my life, okay?"

I nod, not trusting myself to speak yet.

"And how on earth can you possibly think I'm the only person who needs you? When Wish's friend had that accident, and Wish was all messed up over it, who did he call first? Out of everyone—his mom? His brother?"

I find my voice. "Me."

"That's right. He needed you. And when I called you a few minutes ago, what did he need?"

"He needed me to put him first."

"And you answered anyway, in case it was an emergency?"

"It's been us, as friends, for more than twenty years. The worrying about each other and checking up on each other—it doesn't stop because you're getting married."

"Right. I feel the same. But listen—it's okay for him to come first. It's not taking anything away from our friendship for you to love him."

But it *is*. Because answering the phone isn't the only way I've put Ben first. It *is* going to change our friendship.

"This is going to be really hard for me to say. Because it affects you." I have always put him first; Wish was right about that. And putting my needs first—specifically my need to make things right with Wish—is more difficult than I expected.

"Out with it, dude." He pokes my knee. "We don't do small talk."

"There's a good possibility the dealership is going to be closed. If the tax increase goes through. Election Day is a few weeks away." I take a deep breath. "I'm not going to fight it anymore. It's shitty as grand gestures go, but my boyfriend needs that roads project to happen. And I need to put him first."

Ben nods thoughtfully. "That frees me up to help Dave start the wakeboarding camp and cable park he's been talking about building. You should see some of his design ideas for obstacles. They're sick. Hell, is *that* what you were worried about telling me? That I might lose my job?"

A blush creeps up my face.

"Oh, man." He shakes his head. "Dude. I have savings. And besides that, I'm marrying a guy with more money than you. I don't need . . . Come here."

He pulls me into a rough bear hug, his chest heaving. I swallow and push my face into his shoulder, fighting back the tears that have been threatening ever since I walked in. He holds me for a long moment, and then lets me go.

"I love you so much. But you're breaking my heart, man. When I said I didn't need you to take care of me? This is exactly what I was talking about. Move the dealership, close the dealership, do what you gotta do, but don't fight town hall over me."

"You really don't need my help." I sniff, but it's more wonder than sadness. Maybe, more than not being needed, I've been afraid I would be needed and wouldn't be able to be there for him.

"Go make nice with Wish. I put his name on the invitation too, did you see that?"

"Yeah. He's never been to Charleston."

"Neither have I. So we can all do touristy shit down by the Battery together."

"If he comes back. You know, guys his age are exhausting. All this drama."

"He probably says the same about you, you ancient queen."

"Forty-four is not ancient."

"Says the guy who tried to use mascara to cover the gray in his beard."

"That was a secret. If you tell anyone about that, I will—"

"Do something nasty to my spleen. I know. Go apologize to your boyfriend."

"Why were you calling me? When I answered the phone?"

He grins. "To let you know I got the all clear to ride my board again. I thought I'd see if you and Wish wanted to come along with us. But . . . maybe I'll just take Dave and Ridley instead."

After a year of being afraid that this day wouldn't come, that he'd never be able to ride again postsurgery, he's got the all clear. No emergency, just happy news and he wanted to share.

It hurts to miss his first ride, but I realize the wisdom of letting him celebrate with Dave and Ridley.

"I think that would be best. Because right now, he needs me more than you do."

I drive straight to Wish's apartment from Ben's house. I try to call him on the way, but of course he doesn't answer. After our first fight, it took him days to cool down enough to talk to me. But I have the sinking feeling if I give him a cooling-off period, he'll never speak to me again. I figure I can explain, and I'm fully prepared to beg him to listen if I have to. I take the stairs two at a time and pause to catch my breath a moment before knocking on his door.

Trinity opens the door and folds her arms over her chest. "He doesn't want to talk to you."

"I know, but this is important. Can you ask him if he'll just give me a few minutes?"

She glares at me. "They went out."

"Out?" My jaw drops, and I brace myself against the doorway. He was supposed to be here. I would grovel a bit and then we'd live happily ever after, or at least go home and have smokin' hot sex. I wasn't prepared for the possibility he wouldn't be here.

"Out." She looks pointedly out the door. "Not here. And tonight was Jordan and I's anniversary."

I resist the urge to correct her grammar. "I fucked it up good, didn't I?"

"Yeah, you did." She shifts her weight and raises her chin. "You gonna do something about it?"

"You know where they went?" I ask her, mimicking her attitude. A ghost of a smile flickers around her lips.

"You know Champs?"

"The sports bar?" I groan. "Really?"

"Jordan is fine with a gay roommate, but he draws the line at going to gay bars, you know?"

Well, I can certainly appreciate his reticence there, but *ugh*. The worship of grown men chasing a ball is so not *my* scene. Not that I was invited.

"Okay, Trinity, how's this? I get your boyfriend back in time for dinner, and it's on me. Have him take you to the most expensive restaurant in town; I don't care. I'll call and settle the bill, okay?"

She softens a little. "You get your boyfriend back by suppertime too, okay?"

I start back down the stairs, then stop. I look up, and she's watching me, so I call over my shoulder, "How many years?"

"What?"

"You and Jordan. How many years have you been dating?"

"Oh, it's our ten-month anniversary." She gives me a sly smile. "Longer than you and Wish, anyway."

"Go put on a fancy dress and make a restaurant reservation. I'll have him back in time for dinner."

Champs is a neon-covered monstrosity. At one point, the building had been painted that peculiar shade of pink that is bizarrely popular in Central Florida, and then later it was painted over with a dull yellow. In some places, the pink still shows through. The "character" of Lake Lovelace is tired-er here on the west side of town.

I park out front and walk into the dark bar, senses assaulted on all sides by televisions, Jimmy Buffett music, and the smells of beer, sweat, and fried food. I search for Wish, and find him and Jordan in a corner booth. He doesn't see me at first, he's too busy waving his hands at Jordan, but as I approach, he looks up and his face shutters.

"May I join you?" I ask, suddenly sure I'm doing exactly the wrong thing, but it's too late to do anything about it.

Jordan springs to his feet and gets in my face, all fire and venom. "He doesn't want to talk to you. Can't you take a hint? If he wanted to hear anything you had to say, he would have answered his phone."

Okay, yes, brawling is a particular turn-on of mine, but getting my ass kicked by my boyfriend's straight roommate is not foreplay. I hold up my hands in what I hope is a placating gesture.

"It's important." I peer over his shoulder, step to the side, and plead with Wish. He won't even meet my eyes. "Please. I know—I know you're really mad. I don't deserve it, I know I don't, but please listen—I can't let the conversation we had this afternoon be the last thing we ever say to each other."

"Maybe that isn't up to you." Jordan crosses his arms and steps in front of me again.

"Maybe it isn't up to you either," I snap, and attempt to sidestep him. This time he grabs my shirt in his fists and shoves me back.

"Jord, let him go." Wish's voice is almost as wrecked as that day he called me from the hospital. "You're gonna get us kicked out."

Jordan takes a step back.

"Eddie, I can't . . ." Wish drops his gaze to the table.

"Please. Can you honestly say you'll be any more willing to talk to me three days from now?"

"No, I won't." He takes a swig of his beer.

"So hear me out. At least let me apologize for—shit, for everything."

He finally meets my eyes and stares for a long time, making me think for a minute he's going to let his roommate drag me outside to deliver an unholy ass whuppin', but then he says, "Fine."

Jordan moves to sit back down, and I clear my throat. "Um, a little privacy please?"

"I drove."

"I'll drive him home." I smile as sweetly as I can manage. "Shouldn't you be celebrating your anniversary with Trinity?"

"I'll take a cab. Go on, Jord." Wish glances at his friend, then back at me. "You might as well sit."

Jordan glares at me. "Don't be a dick, man."

I laugh, thinking his admonition has probably come too late, but then take his abandoned seat. He and Wish perform some elaborate bro-shake, and he finally leaves.

A half-eaten order of onion rings sits on the table with an empty bottle of Rolling Rock. I push both away, wrinkling my nose. Serious conversation should never be served with a side of fried food.

"Thank you, for letting me stay and talk. I know it's a thing with you, when you're angry, but you can't fix things by running away from them."

"Sometimes I don't want to fix them, and it's easier to walk away."

Those words are like a punch in the face. "I see."

Wish takes a pull on his beer and then waves it at me. "So, let's hear it."

"Hear what?"

"Your argument for how I'm wrong."

"You're not wrong." I shrug. "Well, you're not right either. But you're not wrong. I have some issues with Ben."

"Understatement of the year." He snorts, then picks up one of the onion rings, takes a bite, and scowls at it. "These are terrible, don't eat them."

"I wasn't planning on it." I smile at him.

"Just because I wouldn't wish disgusting food on you doesn't mean I'm falling for your shit, Eddie."

"I'm sorry, Wish. I'm so sorry. This afternoon I was stupid, and I was wrong, and you have every right to be mad at me."

He twirls his finger as if to say *go on*.

"You are *not* my second choice. I want you. I don't want Ben. You're absolutely right that I'm used to putting him first, to trying to make life easier for him. Because he's my friend and I take care of the people I love."

"I knew it." He shakes his head, and his chin trembles a bit. "Goddamn it, Eddie. You gotta do this to me in public?"

"Hey." I cover his hands with my own. "I've been friends with Ben a long time. I love him, yes, but not like . . . not like you."

He flinches, like a feral cat when you hold out food. "Not like me how?"

"Not like you at all." I lift his hand and kiss it. "You, I want to see doing yoga at the foot of my bed every morning, and if you're not there, I miss you. I think about you all the time. You're responsible for goddamn every inappropriate erection I get in the course of my day-to-day. You make me feel young and wild and like everything or anything is possible."

"Yeah, see you say things like that, but your actions don't match up with your words."

"I know, and that's what I'm trying to explain. I put him first this afternoon, out of habit, out of—just years of habit. And I shouldn't have, because he's not that person to me anymore. He's not the person I should put first. You are."

"How can I believe you?" He sniffs, then straightens his spine. "I mean you say this . . . this awesome thing about how I make you feel, and how you're going to put me first, but how do I trust that?"

"I don't know that I deserve your trust. I want it. I want it so badly." I shake my head. "No one has *ever* made me feel this way. And maybe I don't deserve to."

He looks down at our hands, still joined on the table. "So what are you going to do about it?"

"Well, for one, I'm going to stop fighting the roads bill. I'm going to close my dealership if the county votes that way, and I'm going to let Ben move on."

"You really are, aren't you?" Wish studies me over his beer. "What about your other employees?"

"For those I can place elsewhere, I will. For others, temporary unemployment while we rebuild. It's not an ideal situation, but it will get them by."

"What about Keith?"

I shrug. "He's my friend, not my responsibility."

"You're really not in love with him?"

"Keith? No." I shudder. "Straight boys, am I right?"

"I meant Ben."

I shake my head. "I swear."

"I'm falling for you." He glares at me, right in the eye, a sudden ferocity in his voice. "I'm falling *hard*. And I might be a bit of a diva for asking, but I need to come first for you."

I don't hesitate. "You do. And I will do everything I can do to prove it to you."

He sits back in his chair, but his hand is still clasped with mine on the table, so I pull him forward with a gentle tug. "And I'm falling for you too. *Hard*."

His face lights up, and he whispers, "How hard?"

"Let me take you home and I'll show you." I grin.

He laughs, then gets serious. "I'm going to try. Because I want to believe you, and even though I'm scared, I think you mean it."

"I do. With all my heart." Relief washes over me, but also wariness. I might have fucked up, but he hurt me too. "Can we talk about how you walk away from us when you're mad?"

He sits back a little, discomfort clear on his face. "I know I said I didn't want to talk, but I was wrong. It's just that confrontation makes me feel like the worst parts of me are exposed."

"Sometimes being exposed is a good thing. And look, I'm stubborn and used to getting my way, but I wouldn't have pushed so hard if you weren't important to me. It kills me that you would rather walk away than fix this."

"I think you and I are worth fixing—I shouldn't have said that I didn't want to fix it. I'm sorry. If you hadn't come after me, I would have let being pissed at you ruin the best thing in my life."

"Best thing in my life too," I admit. "Can you try to do this for me: talk through our problems instead of storming off when you get mad?"

"I might need you to force the issue—I'm not good at this part."

"It's a deal," I promise him. "So. Can we go back to talking about how hard you make me?"

chapter THIRTEEN

election Day fills me with the same dread I used to get before exams in school. Nail-biting, gut-clenching nerves. I wake up the first time at 3 a.m., toss and turn for an hour before Wish pulls me against the hard heat of his body and shushes me. Somehow, in his arms, I relax enough to fall back to sleep, and by the time I wake again, he's gone to work.

The coffee in the pot is still warm, and there's a note next to my mug.

Max invited us to dinner tonight. Text me later if you want to go.

If my plans, my efforts to stop the bill, bear fruit, he might have to move. Away from Max. Away from his mom. Chase a job to another part of the state—or another state altogether. I feel sick at the thought of what I may have cost him. And, of course, he'd also be moving away from me. How ironic I once feared tying a younger man to my older, settled lifestyle, and now I'm afraid I may have driven him from it?

One way or another, the results of today's vote will change everything for me. I'll either keep my dealership, potentially losing my boyfriend, or I'll lose the dealership and pro shop. As much as both prospects sting, it isn't the idea of not being Ben's boss anymore that woke me up in the middle of the night.

I take my coffee to the back patio and watch the breeze stir the lake. A fisherman trolls by in his low flatboat, and I want to shout at him that it isn't fair for him to be out enjoying himself while my life is a mess. It's not often I've been presented with a situation I can't control, and I hate the way helplessness chokes me, squeezes me. I wave to him instead, and he waves back.

Civilized, on the surface at least.

Later that morning, I head to Lake Lovelace High School—remodeled since the days when I brightened its hallways with my matriculation—my assigned polling place. The same hallways where I claimed my queerness so no one could use it against me seem dark and tiny and a little smelly now. The gym, with its array of high-tech voting machines and its crew of senior citizen volunteers, proudly proclaims its status as home to the Lake Lovelace Lions.

I take my place standing in line behind a mom who's struggling to contain two young kids in a big double stroller. She's the first person I've seen today displaying the same turmoil I feel. I can almost smell the desperation coming off her as she lifts the smaller baby and tries to stick a pacifier in its crying mouth. The baby only cries harder and spits the pacifier on the floor. Whatever they say about misery loving company must be true, because I take an immediate liking to the mom. I wonder how she's planning to vote. Would a wider bridge make any difference in her life? I pick up the pacifier and hand it back to her.

"I'm sorry," she says to me, an edge of panic in her voice. "She's teething."

"She's adorable," I reassure her, and her face brightens.

"Thank you." She maneuvers the baby's fist into the squalling mouth, and the crying stops. The mom's shoulders slump in relief. A voting machine opens, and she wheels her kids over to it with a last apologetic smile over her shoulder.

Another voting machine opens, and I go do what I can to choose my fate. It's not easy to let Romeo win. I know, here in this voting booth, nobody can see which way I vote. I could walk out, say anything I wanted, and no one would be the wiser. But there's only one way I can possibly vote and still like myself afterward.

When it's done, even though it's illegal, I snap a picture of my ballot—and my vote in favor of the tax increase—and send it to Wish, with a note:

Yes to dinner.

I don't get his reply until I'm driving to work, and I don't check it until I pull up in front of the marina. When I look at the screen, his answer brings a smile to my face.

For me? <3 Thank you.

Max opens the door, claps me on the shoulder, and invites me inside. I hand Carrie the vase of lilies I brought with me, and she smiles and fusses over them as though no one ever gave her a hostess gift before. She sets them on the table, a bright-pink centerpiece, and turns to me.

"Wish is in the backyard manning the grill. You want a beer?"

"Sure."

She disappears into the kitchen and returns a moment later with a cold bottle of Sam Adams. I thank her and take in my surroundings.

The house is a small ranch, with the kitchen and dining area on one side of the entryway, and the living room on the other. A hallway to one side leads to the garage, and another on the other side to the bedrooms. The whole house could fit in one corner of mine, but it's everything mine isn't: inviting, cozy. I cross through the living area to the sliding glass door, open it, and step out onto a concrete-slab patio. Kelly, reading a book in a hammock in the backyard, waves to me, and I return the wave. Wish, wearing nothing but a pair of khaki shorts, flip-flops, and a backward baseball cap, grins at me and tugs me into a languid kiss.

"You are my favorite person right now," he says as he pulls away.

"You're mine." I kiss the end of his nose, and he playfully swats at me with the spatula.

"Hey now, none of that with the grill tools," Max admonishes as he follows me through the door. "Polls just closed."

I look down at my watch. Sure enough, it's seven o'clock. I shrug at Wish, trying to appear nonchalant.

"Hey, if it doesn't pass, I'm still gonna try to stay here." He lifts my chin with one finger. "I'm not going anywhere unless I can't find work."

Still, the atmosphere is a little strained over dinner. Carrie has to ask me three times to pass the rolls, as I mull the best way to discuss contingency plans with Wish. Even if he doesn't want to work for me, I have friends who could give him a job. Even a temporary one until another construction project comes through.

"Edward, what are your plans for the dealership if the bill passes? Are you going to move it or close it?" Kelly asks, as if it's simple small talk.

"I haven't decided, actually. I have a significant investment in stock, so moving the dealership is likely, but only if an appropriate property can be developed for a reasonable price. In the meantime, I've got my broker searching for property."

"Seems a shame no matter which way it goes, one of you is screwed," Carrie says, looking back and forth between me and Wish. "I don't envy you."

Wish glares at her. "Eddie and I will work it out. Other relationships have been through worse, you know."

"Sorry, I didn't mean anything by it." She blushes.

"It's okay, sweetheart," I reassure her. "Wish and I are trying to set a record for the highest number of awkward family dinners one relationship can survive."

After dinner, Max asks if we want to play cards, but Wish puts him off, reminding him he needs to work early.

"You're just scared to lose," Max teases.

"More like scared to see you cry when you lose to my big gay boyfriend," Wish teases back.

"Oh, ho!" Max throws a faux punch, and just like that they're wrestling like overgrown puppies.

Kelly rolls her eyes. "Will you two ever grow up?"

"They're hopeless." Carrie sighs, then turns to me. "Want to check the election results? You haven't taken your hand off your phone all night."

"I'm not sure." I shrug. "I don't know if I want to find out with him, or alone."

"Just about everything is better faced together." She smiles at me. "But maybe alone together would be best."

"Can I help you with the dishes?" I ask, deftly pulling a chair out of the way of a flailing leg.

"No, thank you. I'm particular about my kitchen. Max!" She kicks at the flying foot, and both the Carver men sit up, sheepish looks on their faces.

"Sorry." Max stands up and pulls Wish to his feet. "It's a brother thing."

Wish gives Max a one-armed hug. "Sorry," he mutters to Carrie, but I can tell from the way his eyes are sparkling that he doesn't really mean it.

"Well," I start, "thank you for a lovely dinner, but I'm going to head out now. Wish, can I talk to you before I go?"

"If you wait just a minute for me to find my shirt, I'll come with you." He heads off to the back patio, disappears for a moment, then returns, pulling a blue T-shirt over his head and knocking his baseball cap to the floor. He picks it up and gives me a bashful grin as he puts it back on his head. "Ready when you are."

I watch his headlights in my rearview as we head toward the lake, all the way to my driveway. I park the Mercedes inside, and he leaves his truck in the drive, locking up and following me.

It reminds me of that first time, the day I met him, when I stripped for him right there in the garage and then took him inside and let him change my life.

How could I have known a few months ago that he'd become this important to me?

"Wish, how much time is left on your lease at your apartment?"

He stops, cocks his head, and answers me slowly. "Three more months. Then I go month to month until the current project is finished."

"Would you consider moving in here with me instead?"

He stares, his lips moving as he repeats my words silently to himself, then out loud, "Move in with you?"

"Yes. Move in with me. Live with me."

"If the tax increase doesn't pass—I wouldn't be able to pay you rent."

"I don't want—" I stop as his mouth tightens. "I am inviting you to live with me and be my partner. I don't expect you to pay me rent."

He lets out a rough breath. "I don't know. I feel like you're grasping at something to keep me here."

I grip my hands together behind my back so he can't see them shaking.

"How do you know you'll still want me here in three months?" he continues.

I lift my hands up. "Because right now, I can't imagine ever not wanting you with me. If you won't let me give you job security, at least let me give you some other security."

"People would think—"

"Who cares what people think?" I nearly explode. He rocks back on his heels.

"I'm sorry," I say quietly. "I didn't mean to cut you off."

"I need to think about it. I don't . . . Asking me like this tonight . . . it doesn't feel right. I'm sorry. I think if we decide to do that, to move in, that's a big deal. I don't want it to be because you're scared of the future, or because you feel sorry for me, or anything like that. I don't want it to feel like a last resort."

"Why don't you let me do something nice for you?" I plead, taking his hands. "Just let me take care of us."

"I told you, I don't want a daddy. But thank you for thinking of me."

"I thought it was our age difference that would come between us, but it's the money, isn't it?" I feel bitter as I say it, and I don't think it's just that he turned me down. I can't do anything about having been born rich, any more than I can do anything about my age, or the fact that he shares neither.

"I'm not saying never—I'm saying not like this. I'm sorry. I don't want money to come between us, but it's there. You've never not had money."

"I don't see how that's a character flaw," I mutter.

"It's not—I don't resent it, but I don't know how to deal with it. My parents— We were fine, you know, when we were kids. Mom worked part-time so she could be home in the afternoons. There were savings accounts and a couple of vacations." He smiles a little, but it's cynical. "And then there was the divorce. Lawyers, fights over child support and after-school care, and then there wasn't enough money for the things that we used to take for granted. Dad used money as a weapon, because he had it and Mom didn't."

"I would never deliberately hurt you like your father hurt your mother."

He scrubs a hand over his face and looks at me. "I don't want to be *supported*."

"I didn't mean to suggest—"

"I know you didn't. For what it's worth, Eddie, I really want to—to be with you and your piles of money and not feel weird about it."

I nod, turning my head so he can't see the tears glittering in my eyes. "Well, should we check the results?"

"They probably won't be online until morning. Maybe we should just go to bed instead."

It seems like neither of us is quite ready to face it.

I follow him upstairs, and we crawl into bed together. Neither of us makes a move to initiate sex, but he pulls me into the comfortable curve of his body and wraps his arms around me.

"We'll work it out," he whispers.

I nod, feeling his breath tickle my ear, until it slows into a gentle rhythm and he falls asleep. I lie awake a long time, listening to him, feeling him. Memorizing him.

I stare at the election results on my phone. It was close—very close. But the tax increase passed. The roads bill is funded. I flop back in bed and stare at the ceiling. Wish must know already, but he left for work over an hour earlier with a kiss to my forehead and an "I'll call you later."

Anticipating that call fills me with dread.

I'm embarrassed. Oh sure, in the light of day, I can see why he said no when I asked him to move in. I asked him all wrong, and I insulted his sense of self-worth. I know better, and if I'd been thinking clearly, I would have waited. But damn. I want him here. And now I'm going to have to find a way to ask again that doesn't carry with it any aspersions on his independence.

But there's nothing to be done now. He's got three months left on his lease, and that's three months for me to convince him he belongs here with me.

My phone rings. *Keith*. It's hard to commiserate with someone when you feel more relief than misery.

"Hey, sugar." I cover my discomfort with sass.

"Hi, Ed. You hear the news?"

"Yeah. Tough break. But I guess this is what the people want."

He snorts. "Yeah. How about that? Listen buddy, I know you worked hard, and I'm so damned sorry you'll have to close the dealership."

I stifle an awkward laugh. "I'll work it out."

"I figure I'll be raising membership rates slightly, but those who want to will pay it," he says, sounding resigned. "I mean, it's not like this town has a kinky club on every corner, right?"

"Of course. And remember what I said about helping out. I can invest if you need a partner."

"Thanks. Haven't seen you at the club lately. You or the pretty boy you played with last time." If I didn't know him better, I'd take it for an accusation, but no—Keith isn't like that.

"Yeah, about that . . . You were right. I do like him. We've been dating."

"Well, good for you." There's a new warmth in his voice. "Complementary kinks *and* companionship. That's pretty great."

"We're happy." I think. I hope. In spite of last night's faux pas, I really want to believe we are.

"Then I'm happy for you. Well, I only wanted to check and see if you'd heard the news. Want to have dinner sometime soon? Bring your guy."

"I'd like that. I'll call you later in the week to set something up."

"Sounds good. Later, Ed."

"Bye, Keith."

Bring your guy.

I smile. He *is* my guy. And, the roads bill passing means he's more likely to be staying.

I can't complain about that.

chapter FOURTEEN

the following Saturday, sitting in the stands of the Lake Lovelace State University gym, sandwiched between Ben and Wish and watching Tina fight her way on roller skates through a pack of chicks in spandex and fishnets, I can't help but think this is one of the strangest afternoons I've ever spent. The smell of old sweat lingers in the air, and the shouts and whistles are far too reminiscent of high school for my taste. But this is important to Tina, so I lean toward Wish and ask, "Please explain what's happening, one more time?"

"She's the jammer. She gets points for each of the girls in yellow she passes, so they don't want to let her through."

"How can you tell?"

Wish and Ben exchange one of those secret-jock-knowledge glances.

Ben sighs. "The star on her helmet. Plus, she said this morning she's excited we're seeing her first bout as jammer. It's a big deal to her."

He says that like sports talk is even the same language as English. I sit back in my seat and watch her make a break for the outside of a turn and swing past the group who'd been shoving at her. As soon as she's clear, she makes a sprint for it, and people start shouting all around us. Wish and Ben stand up and start shouting along with them, so I stand and whistle and add my voice to the crowd, only sitting when everyone else does.

"See, that was exciting." Ben nudges my arm with his elbow.

"Jocks," I mutter.

When I start to understand how the game is played, it does get exciting, and I'm thrilled to see Tina take a win in her first bout as whatever-they-call-it. Afterward, she comes up to us and gives us each a sweaty hug.

"Ew, girl sweat," I joke, and she laughs.

"I'm so glad you guys made it!"

Ben rubs the side of his face with one finger as he smiles at her. "Dave's sorry he couldn't come. He's in Charleston dealing with wedding stuff. You remember how that goes."

"I do, though, honestly, Lisa took care of most of it. Damn, I can't believe the wedding is two weeks away."

Ben gets that little-boy grin on his face again. "Me neither."

She turns to me. "Well, what did you think, Mr. Anti-Jock? Did you have a good time?"

I give her a sly smile. "I loved watching you have so much fun, but there are more pleasant ways to collect bruises. *Ahem.*"

"It was great, T. You were awesome out there." Wish takes my hand. "But Eddie and I have an appointment in a half hour, so I'm gonna have to steal him."

"We do?" I stare at him. "Since when?"

"Since now. It's a surprise. Say good-bye, Eddie."

"Good-bye, Eddie," I parrot.

Tina and Ben laugh and wave good-bye as Wish pulls me away.

"See you at the wedding, T!" I call back over my shoulder.

"Do we really have an appointment somewhere?" I ask. "Or are you unable to resist my considerable charms?"

"While your charms are—" he looks me up and down, making a big show of checking out my ass "—considerable, we actually do have an appointment. Keys." He holds out his hand, and I drop my keys into it. It turns out, I trust him with my car just fine.

He opens the passenger door for me, then moves around to the driver's seat. "You can say no, hell, you can safeword if you want. But I wanted to do something nice for you, since you're always doing nice stuff for me. And well, you'll see."

Something nice and *safeword*? My curiosity is definitely piqued, and never more so than when he pulls up in front of the piercing studio where I got my dick pierced.

Bemused, I ask, "Are you buying me jewelry for my cock?"

He faces me. "Remember when I said I wished I could have been there when you got your Prince Albert done?"

I shudder, remembering the night on the boat. "Of course. But, lovely, what's done is done."

He reaches out and pinches my nipple, right through my shirt. "But these aren't pierced. What do you say?"

Arousal and anticipation swamp me. I love the idea of a nipple piercing. I love the idea of him watching. But before he gets the idea he can just have his way . . .

"You know, some boyfriends cook dinner when they want to do something nice," I point out.

"I'm a lousy cook. Besides, I've jerked off all week thinking about what kind of face you'll make when the needle goes in."

Okay, that's all the sounding out I need. My dick is hard, my mouth is dry, and my palms are sweating in nervous anticipation.

"I love the idea of you watching me get pierced."

"Do I hear a 'but'?" He takes my hand, playing with my fingers. "If you don't like the way it looks, or if you aren't into the idea, it's . . . it's fine."

"I love the way nipple piercings look. I'm totally into the idea. I'm ridiculously pleased that you thought of it. Here's the but: I love nipple play—so only one. That way we can still play with the other side while that one heals."

He grins and kisses me, then says, "I can't tell you how much it turns me on that you want to do this—you might have noticed I have a kink for marks."

I roll my eyes. "Understatement of the year, lovely."

He flashes that dazzling grin at me. "Okay, so a piercing is like that—a mark—but more permanent than a bruise. And to know that when you see it, you'll think of me. God, that turns me on."

"You know what turns me on?"

He shakes his head.

"That you wanted to do something nice for me and thought of needles. You're perfect. Don't ever change."

There's something oddly intimate about a man's relationship with the woman who pierced his dick. Natasha gives me a big hug and asks how it's working for me, and I manage to give her a completely rational answer about the state of my cock without it being too much information or creepy or anything.

She leads us back into the private room where she does the piercing. "All right, take off your shirt, Ed. I need to see what I'm working with."

The air-conditioning is cold, and my nipples harden and pucker.

"Which side are we doing?"

I turn back to Wish. "Do you have a preference?"

"Left, over his heart."

"Aww, so romantic." Natasha sticks her tongue between her teeth and wrinkles her nose like it's the cleverest thing anyone has ever said. Then she pulls on a glove and starts feeling around my nipple.

"You have nice nipples for a piercing. Should be super easy on you. I recommend using a barbell at first to make sure it doesn't tug at the nipple as it heals. But you can switch to a ring once it's healed up."

She peels off the glove. "I'll go get your jewelry ready; you sit down and get comfortable."

I settle back in the chair and glance over at Wish—half-hard and dying to kiss the smug look off his face. "Come here."

He leans in and kisses me, and I can practically taste the anticipation humming between us. His hand runs up my bare chest and he slides it around behind my neck.

"Oooh, boys, settle down or sell tickets. Shit, that's hot." Natasha returns with her tools and the jewelry on a stainless steel tray. "Everything has been autoclaved." She sets the tray down and crosses to the sink. She washes her hands, puts gloves on, and approaches me, smiling. "Gotta clean you and mark a little dot where the needle goes through. Your nipple will probably get erect from all the handling, so we'll wait a minute so I can check the placement on an unerect nipple. When we're ready to go, I'll put a clamp on your nipple, have you take a deep breath in and let it out slowly. As you let it out, I'll pierce the nipple, then pull the barbell through. Any questions?"

"Will it hurt, Tash?" I make my eyes huge and put a tremble in my voice.

"You'll love it," she promises.

While she gets my nipple ready, Wish watches her with a fascinating mix of curiosity and arousal on his face. He catches me staring at him and laughs. "What?"

"Nothing. You're freaked out and turned on; it's surprisingly hot."

"I've never seen anyone get anything pierced before. I'm like a kid in a candy store trying to play it cool."

I laugh.

"You can hold his hand while I do it. Putting the clamp on now, it might pinch a bit."

It does pinch, but no worse than the clothespins or a nipple clamp. I take a few deep breaths. Even though this was his idea of doing something nice for me, it feels right, somehow to show him a permanent sign of my affection.

"Deep breath in," Natasha says, and I look up at Wish's face.

As the needle pushes through me, there's a moment of agony that makes me gasp and pinch my eyes shut, then a rush of blood in my ears, and Wish smiling down at me, his eyes dark with lust. *Holy shit.*

"Jewelry." A quick tug, then Natasha steps back to admire her work. "Nice. It's a good look for you. Can you stand up?"

I nod, but Wish helps me anyway, and he leads me over to the mirror, where he stands behind me, rubbing my arms and studying my face in the mirror.

"That was the hottest thing I've ever seen," he whispers.

It was definitely the most intense piercing experience I've ever had. With him watching, it was like foreplay. Judging by the bulge prodding my ass, he feels the same.

"Let's settle up here and go home."

"Fuck, yeah."

chapter FIFTEEN

the morning of Ben's wedding, I wake up on lush hotel sheets with late-fall sunlight streaming through floor-to-ceiling windows and Wish wrapped around me like a blanket.

I roll to my side to find him already awake, staring at me.

"That is so creepy," I tell him, a smile twitching at my lips. He grins back and kisses me, rubbing our hips together.

"Hmm. Never mind, that's not creepy, not creepy at all." I gasp as he slides a hand down to cup my ass and pull us closer. His motions are jerky, rough and quick. There's an urgency to his frotting, a sort of desperation I'm not used to first thing in the morning, and no lie, it's hot in its enthusiasm. Who doesn't love to be wanted like that? I push harder against him, tilt my hips to change the angle, and hold tight as he comes against my belly. He reaches down and uses the warm slickness of his cum to jerk me to my own orgasm.

In the aftermath, my head on his shoulder, his hand resting on my stomach, I ask, "What was that for? I mean, it was fun, but intense, you know?"

"I thought you might wake up stressed this morning."

"Uh-huh." I tease, "You wanted to make me smell like you. Staking your claim." I sit up and toss a pillow at him. "Shoulda waited until after the shower."

He laughs, his face flushing with pleasure. "Who says I won't?"

The hotel shower is one of those big glass enclosures with three different showerheads. I pull him in behind me and start to wash him under the spray, pausing to kiss and nibble and lick all my favorite parts of his body, and then he does the same, careful not to bump or prod the barbell in my nipple as he washes around it. Neither of us gets hard again, and it's a different intimacy, washing each other, appreciating each other, without sex as the endgame. It catches at me, the poignancy of it, and I find myself shaking as I rinse the shampoo from his hair.

"You okay?" he asks, grabbing my trembling hand and nibbling at it.

I nod, a lump forming in my throat. "I was standing here, thinking how nice it is to be with you like this, and how good it feels, and it just hit me that I'm crazy about you."

He runs his hand through my wet hair and wraps an arm around my waist, like we're dancing. "I'm crazy about you too."

The wedding ceremony isn't until 6 p.m., but there's brunch and photographs, and I can't seem to get Ben alone until right before the main event. He's like a stranger in his gray suit with a peach-colored tie and a sea grass rosette pinned to the lapel, but then he smiles at me, a big goofy grin, and we both start laughing.

"I'm really, really happy for you, Brawny."

"Thanks, man." He opens his arms, and I walk into them and give him a huge hug. "That means a lot to me. Did you ever think, back when we were kids, we'd be able to do this?"

"No. I still can't believe it's real, actually. Big queer weddings. I never." I clutch my tie like it's a string of pearls, then sober up. "But I'm so glad. Because I don't think you've ever been this happy, and it thrills me to see it. I really want you to know that. After everything, you being this happy—it's awesome."

He makes a little show of straightening something on my suit jacket—which I happen to know is pristine as fuck—but I let him anyway, and then he hugs me again and I figure the emo-talk is over for now.

"Hey, Ed," Dave says behind me. "Can I steal my husband-to-be away?"

"Of course, Bedhead." I turn to face him, and he's freckled and smiling, with his hair tamed into something almost orderly. "He's all yours. I think it's time to show Ben's mama to her seat."

Ben groans. "Don't let her get talking. She's still on about how she doesn't know why it has to be called 'marriage,' and can't we all just call it something else so no one gets confused." He mimics his mama's Southern drawl with a practiced ear and a flair for the absurdity of her remark. I roll my eyes. I can hear it now.

"At least she's here," Dave says quietly enough that I don't think I was supposed to hear it, and I take my leave before my reaction can show on my face. To Dave's knowledge, his family—at least his mother and his stepbrother—aren't here, and their absence is clearly weighing on him. There was no way Romeo would ever let his son travel out of state to a gay wedding.

Dave doesn't know that Ridley came to my office after Election Day with a plan to thwart his parents and come to the wedding anyway. I feel an anticipatory thrill, knowing that Ridley and his friend Caden arrived at the hotel just after brunch. His plan had given me an opportunity to stick it to his dad while doing something nice for Dave and Ben. A win-win all around. I couldn't wait to see Dave's face when he saw his brother.

For all her lack of political support, Ben's mother loves her son enough to be here for him, and when I hold out my arm, she takes it with a big smile.

"I always figured he'd end up with you," she says in a stage whisper, poking me in the chest with one peach-painted fingernail. "Shows what this old lady knows."

"Why, Mrs. Warren, we all know I'm too much of a bad influence on a good boy like Ben." I wink at her, and she laughs.

"Well, I don't reckon you turned out so bad," she concedes.

Across the aisle, young and awkward and immensely pleased with himself, Ridley is settling Dave's aunt—his dad's sister—into her seat. He catches my eye, and I give him a little nod. We go take our places by the officiant and wait. I search for Wish out among the guests and find him halfway back, watching me. I give him a surreptitious smile, and he answers it with one of his own.

Then the music starts.

Ben and Dave walk down the aisle together, hand in hand, and the moment Dave sees Ridley is something I'm not likely to ever forget. He startles, looks like he's going to cry, then wipes the back of his hand across his eyes and nods, like a major problem is solved and everything is all right now. And I guess it is. Ben leans in and whispers something to Dave, and they both turn to each other and grin.

They don't stop grinning at each other throughout the ceremony, and by the time they get to the kiss, answering grins spread throughout the guests. Ben's mama lets out a wolf whistle, his dad tries to shush her, and everyone bursts into laughter and applause.

Ben leans his forehead against Dave's for a long moment, eyes closed, then tugs his hand and leads him back down the aisle. Ridley and I follow, and it hits me, really hits me: Ben is married, and I'm nothing but happy.

There's something about the silly half-drunk people get at wedding receptions that makes me smile. Ben, of course, is drinking soda, but the wine flows freely, and when Davis pulls me into a dance, I've got my own buzz working. He's taller than me and, like me, clearly suffered through ballroom dance lessons at some point. I giggle when he pulls me into the classic form and starts to lead me through a fox-trot, which devolves to a sloppy, overly lewd rumba when Ben whistles at us.

"Thank you so much for being here," Dave murmurs against my ear. "It means the world to both of us."

I squeeze him around the waist and give him a teasing grope. "It means a lot to me too."

"I think we wouldn't be here today if it hadn't been for you. And what you did for Ridley? So he could be here? I can't tell you—" He breaks off and sniffs, his steps faltering.

"Oh, no, Bedhead. No tears, I am not equipped to handle that today." I take the lead and pull him into a turn. "What did Ben say to you, halfway down the aisle? Made you grin like a fool?"

Dave laughs. "He said 'I'm flying.'"

"I'm flying? What the hell does that mean?"

Dave grins at me, and then spins me under his arm. "It means I love him. And he knows it."

"Y'all have some weird-ass inside jokes." I shake my head and give him a side-eye for good measure, but then I see Wish talking to Ben across the dance floor, both of them watching us with grins on their faces, and I think I've got a good idea what he means.

When the song ends, we make our way over to them, and I take Wish's hand. "Come walk with me."

His hand is warm and firm in mine, and I give it a little squeeze of appreciation. It's a balmy night for November, and as we walk out onto the plantation grounds, a cool breeze catches the Spanish moss in the trees, making it sway and rustling the last few oak leaves to the ground.

"You did it," he says. "You let him go. First the dealership, now the wedding."

"He was never mine to let go." I look over at him. "You ever see yourself doing something like this?"

"Get married?" He glances back at the lantern-lit dance floor and shrugs, but his face is wistful. "My mom would like that. But I don't think it's my thing."

Thank God for that. I don't know what I'd say next if he professed to dreaming about his wedding day since he was old enough to walk two G.I. Joes down an imaginary aisle.

"What about moving in with someone?" I nudge his hip with our hands. "Someone who loves you, and wants you in his home because it feels more like home with you there. Someone like me."

He stills, turns to me. "Someone who loves me?"

I nod. "I love you. I know I asked you before and you said no, and I hope it was because the way I asked you was wrong, and not because you don't want to be with me. Because I want you with me, and I want you to want to be there, and . . . and I'm going to shut up now because I'm doing this babbling thing I do when I'm nervous and I'm sure it's not very flattering."

His grin is dazzling, even in the dark. "I love you too. And I want to be with you all the time. But . . ."

"Wait," I stop him. "Before you give me an answer—same as before, I don't expect to treat it like a roommate situation. But however you want to contribute to our household expenses, I'll accept graciously. I understand and respect why that's important to you."

"So romantic, S-Class," he teases. "How is a guy supposed to resist a proposal like that?"

"I'm serious." Please, let him see how serious.

"I know you are. I know. And I appreciate that you'll let me contribute. It feels—I don't know. It just feels better. Thank you."

"Is that a yes?" I dare to hope.

"Yes, I'll move in with you."

"Thank God." I pull him into a kiss, breaking it only to say, "I didn't know how I was going to ask a third time if you told me no again."

"I don't ever want to say no to you again," he murmurs against my lips.

I hold his hand as we walk back to the wedding reception, giddy with relief that he said yes, excitement at the idea of living with him—not only the nights of sweaty kinky sex or enjoying the view of his downward-facing dog first thing in the morning, but also having him in my big tacky house to make me feel wild and alive like no one else ever has.

"What are you smiling about?"

"I think running my car off the road this summer might be the best thing that ever happened to me," I confess.

He laughs a little. "Masochist."

"Now with a live-in sadist." I squeeze his hand.

"For as long as you want me." He squeezes back.

"Does forever sound okay?" Oh that was cheesy—I can't believe I actually said it, and I am going to die of embarrassment.

He doesn't laugh. He gives me that little crooked grin, brushes his hair out of his eyes, and nods.

"Yeah, S-Class. That works for me."

And then there's no more talking, and I don't ever want to stop kissing him.

Dear Reader,

Thank you for reading Vanessa North's *Rough Road*!

We know your time is precious and you have many, many entertainment options, so it means a lot that you've chosen to spend your time reading. We really hope you enjoyed it.

We'd be honored if you'd consider posting a review—good or bad—on sites like **Amazon, Barnes & Noble, Kobo, Goodreads, Twitter, Facebook, Tumblr,** and your blog or website. We'd also be honored if you told your friends and family about this book. Word of mouth is a book's lifeblood!

For more information on upcoming releases, author interviews, blog tours, contests, giveaways, and more, please sign up for our weekly, spam-free newsletter and visit us around the web:

Newsletter: tinyurl.com/RiptideSignup
Twitter: twitter.com/RiptideBooks
Facebook: facebook.com/RiptidePublishing
Goodreads: tinyurl.com/RiptideOnGoodreads
Tumblr: riptidepublishing.tumblr.com

Thank you so much for Reading the Rainbow!

RiptidePublishing.com

acknowledgments

I owe a debt of gratitude to those who helped me muscle this book into shape. To Sarah Frantz Lyons for poking me from time to time while I worked through several false starts. To Chris and Liz for medical consulting. And to Caz—many times over—for helping me shape the words I thought I meant into the words I meant to say.

ALSO BY Vanessa north

Double Up (A *Lake Lovelace* novella)
Two in Winter
Fight or Flight
Jackson's Law
Hostile Beauty
The Dark Collector
High and Tight
The Lonely Drop

The Ushers Trilogy
Amazon
United
Cracked

The Wiccan Haus
Shifter's Dance
Shifter's Song

Wild at Heart: Storm Haven
Under a Moonlit Night: Ripped Awake
Lucky's Charms: Seamus
Love in the Cards: Two of Wands

ABOUT THE author

Author of over a dozen novels, novellas, and short stories, Vanessa North delights in giving happy-ever-afters to characters who don't think they deserve them. Relentless curiosity led her to take up knitting and run a few marathons "just to see if she could." She started writing for the same reason. Her very patient husband pretends not to notice when her hobbies take over the house. Living and writing in Northwest Georgia, she finds her attempts to keep a quiet home are frequently thwarted by twin boy-children and a very, very large dog.

Website: vanessanorth.com
Twitter: twitter.com/vanessanwrites
Facebook: facebook.com/authorvanessanorth
Goodreads: tinyurl.com/VNonGR

Enjoy more stories like *Rough Road* at RiptidePublishing.com!

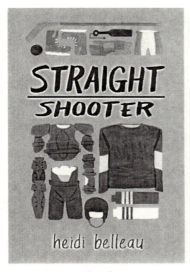

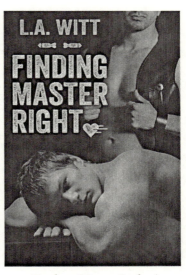

Straight Shooter
ISBN: 978-1-62649-090-1

Finding Master Right
ISBN: 978-1-62649-054-3

Earn Bonus Bucks!

Earn 1 Bonus Buck for each dollar you spend. Find out how at RiptidePublishing.com/news/bonus-bucks.

Win Free Ebooks for a Year!

Pre-order coming soon titles directly through our site and you'll receive one entry into a drawing to win free books for a year! Get the details at RiptidePublishing.com/contests.

CPSIA information can be obtained at www.ICGtesting.com
Printed in the USA
LVOW11s1601140615

442423LV00006BA/788/P